CONTENTS

ACKNOWLEDGMENTS

Editing by Nicola Markus
Qualified Freelance Editor & IPEd Member
nicola@nicolamarkusedits.com

1 VACATION

"I can't wait to get there," said Tibi, looking to his right at Mia.

"Me too. And I'm hungry. As soon as we check in, we can go to that restaurant down the street."

"I checked the menu online. They serve good vegetarian food. We should be fine," said Tibi, checking the GPS on his phone, which was currently fixed onto his Hyundai's dashboard. "We should be there in an hour, if the traffic doesn't get any worse."

"Yeah, we're all good," said Mia, reaching for the radio. "Can I switch this? I hate these songs. Too commercial."

Half an hour later, the road narrowed and began to climb toward the mountains.

"This part of the route is always congested. Let's hope we left early enough," said Tibi, checking his GPS once more. "It looks fine, I think."

"It's almost noon," said Mia. "People will be heading out to eat. It will get crowded soon."

"By the way, did you call in advance?"

"For what?"

"For reservations."

"Yeah, I told you," said Mia. "They said no problem."

"You booked for seven nights, right?"

"No."

"What? Why not?"

"I told you yesterday. Weren't you listening?"

"I was playing on my PC. You know I don't hear things when I'm in the game."

"Yeah, true. You were. So, I called yesterday. They said the guesthouse is almost empty this time of year. So, no need for a reservation; they have plenty of rooms."

"Perfect."

* * *

The small, light-blue sedan took a left, off the national road and onto a small, steep road going up the mountain. It continued for a few hundred yards, then took a 120° right before continuing its ascent.

They entered a cozy little village. Wooden houses lined the road left and right, each one or two stories high. It was a cute resort, surrounded by tall pine trees. All around, mountain peaks towered over the settlement, making it appear as if it were surrounded by giants.

"Look, Tibi, the restaurant we talked about," said Mia, pointing to the right.

"Nice. We'll come here after we check in. Ah, and look, the guesthouse," he said, pointing to their left.

The Three Bears guesthouse was taller than most of the buildings around it. It had a ground floor and two stories on top, and it was painted dark brown. It stood close to the road, but with enough space in front for a small parking lot.

They turned right onto the premises. You could fit four cars in front of the guesthouse, while along the right-hand side of the building, they could see about eight more parking spots, surrounded by a metal mesh fence. A luxury sedan was already parked in front of the guesthouse, but the other three spots were free.

Tibi and Mia got out of the car and stretched; then Tibi went to open the trunk.

He was a relatively short man in his mid-twenties, completely bald, yet with a large beard. He was athletic, rather muscular, and his skin was a shade darker than Mia's.

2

She was taller than him, svelte and sporty, with short blonde hair and a delightful smile. She seemed a few years younger than Tibi, but that might have been the strong summer sun accentuating her natural beauty.

They grabbed one backpack and a duffel bag each and climbed the four steps to reach the lobby.

There was a small counter to the right, where a young man of average height stood next to a tall chair. Ahead was a narrow flight of stairs, and right next to them, a corridor. To the left, just in front of the stairs, was a door with '1' written on it. Near the counter, on the right-hand side of the lobby, was another door marked '2', while in the back, into the corridor, there appeared to be a third room. Everything looked pleasant, clean and fresh.

The man at the counter was looking through a notebook. He appeared to be in his early thirties, yet he was dressed like a fifty-year-old. His brown hair was straight and combed to the side, his face clean-shaven.

Tibi approached the counter. "Good day. I'm Tibi," he said, smiling briefly. "We'd like to book a room. We called, but we were told you had plenty of rooms available, so we didn't make a reservation."

"Yes, Mr. Coman," the man at the counter said in an incredibly high-pitched, sharp voice. "The guesthouse is empty really."

"Indeed, my name is Tiberiu Coman, but everybody calls me Tibi. What do you mean empty?" asked Tibi. "Is there something wrong? Everything looks to our liking."

"No, no," said the young man, waving his hands. "On the contrary. We finished renovating and redecorating half a year ago," said the man, glancing around. "But it's Sunday, so everybody has left to head back to the city. You're simply the first to arrive from the new batch of visitors. But still, there are fewer tourists looking for accommodation during the early weeks of summer."

"Ah, yes," said Mia. "We planned to spend a week here, and then we'll go to the seaside for another week. We try to keep away from the crowds and avoid the traffic."

"Yeah, we like to be a bit off-season," said Tibi. "I hate driving bumper to bumper."

"Right," said the man. "How long will you be staying?"

"Seven nights," said Mia.

"Perfect. Now, I will come with you, to—"

"Can we get a room with a view toward the mountain to the back, but also overlooking the main street? I love these cute little mountain villages, especially at night."

"You may choose whichever room you want," said the man at the counter. "That's what I was trying to say: I will come with you to show you the options."

"Oh, nice," said Tibi, grabbing his duffle bag. "Let's go."

As the man behind the counter emerged, heading for the stairs, another man, probably close to his forties, appeared from behind the stairs, having come down the corridor.

"Hello," he said, with a brief, polite smile. He was dressed in expensive clothes; clearly in a different class to the man serving behind the counter.

"Hi," said Mia and Tibi at the same time.

"Welcome to our guesthouse," said the older man, trying another brief smile. He was average height, yet taller than Tibi, and well groomed. His black hair showed a few white strands and he had a large lower lip. "Emi, show them around."

"Yes, Mr. Horza," said the young man. "Come. I don't think you'll want a room to the ground floor, right? Let's see the first floor."

They climbed the first flight of stairs, up to the landing, and then turned toward the second flight. They slowed for a moment, admiring the wide lobby in front of them. Then they climbed the second flight, reaching the hall there.

"Ah, here it is," said Emi, indicating the way.

There were six doors, all opened and with keys in the locks: two on the left side, two up front, and two to the right. They were numbered eleven to sixteen.

Behind the doors, they could see six corridors. Those of the four rooms on the sides—11, 12, 15 and 16—led to a bathroom. While for rooms 13 and 14, the corridors led directly to the bedroom.

"We can choose any room?" asked Mia, looking around.

"Yes," said Emi. "Any of them."

"Great," said Mia, in a happy tone. "Let's check them all out."

"No," said Tibi. "I don't know, but I feel like the second floor would be better."

"But don't you want to see these rooms first?"

"No. Let's go to the second floor."

"Okay," said Mia, and they all turned back toward the stairs. "By the way, this looks really nice," she added, indicating their surroundings.

"Oh, yes," said Emi in his squeaky voice. "I did quite a lot of the work myself."

"Really?" asked Tibi. "You know your way around the paint roller?"

"Oh, that's simple," said Emi, smiling proudly. "I did most of the drywall, worked on the plumbing, the ceramic tiles. All that."

"Wow, nice," said Tibi as they moved toward the stairs. He searched for another topic of conversation, as the silence while climbing the stairs felt a bit awkward. "The other guy, did he also help?" he eventually asked.

"He's the owner," Emi whispered. "And no. He's useless when it comes to *anything* related to building houses, fixing installations or renovating interiors. Without me, this place would still look like an old barn. Oh, we're here," he added, now in a louder voice.

On the second floor, all the doors were open as well, except for one to the right. In rooms 21 to 25, they saw the same corridors, in a similar layout to those on the first floor.

"This one," said Tibi, pointing at the closed door. "Let's see this room."

"Twenty-six?" asked Emi.

"Yup."

"Of course," he said, going to the right and opening the door.

They entered the long corridor. To the left, the wall was lemon-yellow. To the right, the wall was red with a narrow yet tall window. Tibi took a few steps forward and looked out the window, seeing the forest ascending right behind the guesthouse and a snowy mountain top in the distance.

Up front, at the end of the corridor, was a bathroom. The door was open, and Tibi could see a bathtub and a small window, also open.

To the left of the bathroom was a large archway. Tibi took a few more steps and stopped below the arch. He looked around the large room. A lot of red, bright and strong, covered the lower three-quarters of each wall, except the lemon-yellow one, which from that angle looked wider than expected. A king-size bed, made up with red linen stood at the center of the right wall and, to the left, a long console covered the entire wall. On top was a big flat-screen TV, and to the sides were two small, flimsy chairs with tall backrests. Finally, on the other side of the room, large windows filled almost the entire wall. To the left, near the TV console, there was a door, which probably led to a balcony.

"We'll take it!" said Tibi, turning around with a sparkle in his eyes.

"But don't you want to see the other—"

"No, it's fine," said Tibi, dropping his bag. "This one will do."

"Okay," said Emi. "Let's go downstairs and sign some papers then."

* * *

"They chose twenty-six," said Emi, reaching the counter.

Horza threw a quick glance toward Emi. He took a deep breath, then quickly recovered.

"You were so fast," he said flatly.

"Well, we went in and chose one."

"So you went for twenty-six, just like that?" said Horza, looking deep into Tibi's eyes.

"Well… yes. I mean, I had a good feeling about it."

"Okay," said the manager, shrugging. Then he handed over a sheet of paper. He continued in a colder tone, "Sign this. We lock the front door at 10pm, so you'll need to press the doorbell if you want in after that. Enjoy your stay."

* * *

"What the hell was that?" Mia whispered as the two of them climbed the stairs.

"You saw that too?" asked Tibi, looking at her.

"Yes! It was weird. Okay, he's not the friendliest person, but his expression changed when Emi said we had chosen twenty-six."

"Right! I saw it. Then he was so cold at the end. What was that all about?"

"I don't know. But I didn't like it."

"Maybe something bad happened in this room?" said Tibi as he entered, moving aside so Mia could follow. "What if someone died in here, or, even worse, what if—"

"Stop it!" said Mia as Tibi closed the door behind her. "You know I don't like those sorts of topics."

"Yes, I know. Sorry. I just let my mind fly. But what about Emi's voice? Man, he sounds like a child."

"The poor guy," said Mia. "I heard him over the phone, when I called. At first, I thought it was a lady. I think I even called him 'miss' at first, until he told me his name. Anyway, I imagine it would be difficult for a guy to sound like that."

"Probably," said Tibi, shaking his head. "I hope the voice is his only issue."

"What do you mean?"

"Meaning that he's otherwise healthy. Come on. Let's freshen up and then let's go eat. I'm starving."

* * *

"Ugh," said Tibi, pulling out the ringing phone. "It's Mike."

They were in the local restaurant, the one they'd seen upon entering the charming village, waiting for their food.

"Hey, Mike, how are you?"

"Hey man. How's it going?" Mike spoke so loudly, Mia could almost hear everything.

"Nothing much. Waiting for our food. What's up?"

"Ah, so you had to tell them you're in the lowest part of the food chain?"

"Ha, ha, never heard that one before. Yanking my chain for being vegetarian, are you?"

"No, no. Just, you know, you're basically some sort of bald goat."

"Okay," said Tibi, smiling. "What do you want?"

"Okay, back to business. The director called."

"Which one?"

"*The* one. He needs the design for our game's rewards menu. Did you do it before leaving?"

"Yeah, of course. It's on the server. I checked it in on Friday."

"Okay, cool," said Mike. "I'll look it up. Say hi to Mia. I hope she wears the pants and actually likes meat."

"Depends what you mean by that."

Mike laughed so loudly through the phone that Tibi had to move it a few inches away from his ear. "Good one. Okay, have a pleasant vacation, man. See you in two weeks."

"Yeah, see ya."

"Why did he call?" asked Mia, smiling after hearing Mike's laughter.

"Eh, some design doc. The directors are on fire, apparently."

"What's the deadline for finishing the game?"

"We have Alpha in six months. We finish it in a year and a half, but making games means no one gets a break, apparently."

"Yeah, they should leave you alone. You're on vacation. And what was that laughter all about?"

"You know. Mike and his stupid jokes."

"It sounded like it was your joke," said Mia, grinning.

"Ah, here it comes," said Tibi, seeing the waiter approach with their food.

* * *

"We always do that," said Mia, scoffing as they left the restaurant. "Each time we go to a place for the first time, we order way too much food. We'll need to walk for three hours just to burn off a quarter of those calories."

"Yeah, let's walk," said Tibi, carrying the doggy bag. "Shall we go up the road, see what's there?"

"If we follow the road up, through the village, we'll just reach a dead end. But that's where the cable car station is, the one that can take us up the mountain. Maybe we'll go for a ride tomorrow. But for now let's just walk uphill for a while."

* * *

As evening came, they decided to eat the rest of the food in their room. Then Tibi pulled out a bottle of red wine.

"Can I interest you in some of this?" he asked, waving the bottle around.

"Oh, mister game designer," said Mia, moving next to Tibi and kissing him, "you do know how to treat a lady."

"Well," said Tibi, trying a British accent, "you know I'm the Eastern European Duke of Lordly Behavior."

"Ha, ha," said Mia, kissing him again. "Now *that's* an impressive title. What else can you do?"

"As soon as I open this bottle," said Tibi, interrupted by Mia's kisses, "I will show you."

* * *

"This is a good wine," said Mia, taking another sip. They were both in the bed, under the covers, watching a random movie on TV.

"Yup, not bad," said Tibi, kissing her briefly. "I have one more bottle, but it's in the trunk with the sea-side luggage. Maybe we can buy some more wine tomorrow."

"Yeah, I love red wine," said Mia. "Should we go to sleep? Tomorrow will be a long day."

"What?" said Tibi, reaching over to place his glass on the nightstand. "You think you can get away that easy?"

"Oh, no," said Mia, giggling as Tibi started to kiss her.

* * *

"Goodnight," said Tibi an hour later, turning off his nightstand lamp.

"Goodnight," mumbled Mia, who already seemed to be half asleep.

As darkness engulfed the room, Tibi realized he needed to make a few adjustments, as their room seemed to be surrounded by street lights.

"Damn this light," he mumbled, looking for a solution.

He was on the left-hand side of the bed, the one near the archway. He could see the large opening leading to the corridor. He couldn't see the narrow window from the bed, but it seemed there was plenty of light coming from it, as the corridor looked bright.

To the right, light also invaded the room through the large balcony door and windows. And something was shining right in his eyes.

He got up and looked out the window. A few lampposts stood across the lovely street. Their room was between two of them, yet they seemed to be right at the level of their second floor windows. Tibi pulled the curtains across, trying to block out the light.

Happy with the result there, he moved to the corridor. He looked out the narrow window, only to see a lamppost a few dozen feet away, shining brightly. It was behind the house, lighting the backyard and probably the parking lot on the side of the guesthouse. He could see a few yards away, into the woods and the neighboring backyards.

There was no curtain on that window, however, so, with a sigh, Tibi went back to bed.

He turned to his favorite sleeping position, on his left side, his back to the balcony, and closed his eyes.

* * *

A deep growl woke him. He opened his eyes.

He was looking straight at the opening leading to the corridor behind the thick yellow-toned wall.

Suddenly, he saw a shadow. The corridor was only lit by the street lamp outside the tall window, but that was clearly a large hand emerging from the corridor, reaching around to touch the side of the yellow wall.

A cold sweat ran down Tibi's back, making him flinch.

The shape of a head then appeared, moving slowly, like it was trying to look inside the room.

And soon a body followed.

Tibi let out a yell that he could no longer control.

The silhouette paused for a few seconds that seemed like hours, then slowly pulled back.

The corridor was empty; there was no one there.

What the hell was that? he thought, not having the courage to turn his face away from the opening.

"Mia?" said Tibi in a faint voice. "Mia, are you sleeping?"

Silence. He grabbed his phone with shaky hands and checked the time. It was about twenty minutes past three.

"Hey, Mia," he said in a louder voice. "Can you hear me?"

What if she's under a spell? What the hell was that? Is there someone inside our room? But he was so tall!

Indeed, the shadow's head had been high up, right under the archway.

"Damn," he said out loud.

Mia's not waking. She's in a deep sleep, so she must be very tired. But it was just a bad dream. I must have snored, and my brain took that snore as a growl, waking me up.

Seeing strange things when waking up is normal. You dream so profoundly, and then, as you wake, they disappear. Only this time they didn't disappear. No, the shadow came forward, stopped, looked inside, then went away the way it came. Slowly.

He shifted in the bed, taking a few deep breaths.

This is the strange part: that it didn't disappear the moment I opened my eyes. The moment I became afraid and my adrenalin spiked, it should have disappeared. Why did it continue to move, like a shadow?

Tibi shook his head. This was all just a bad dream. He'd had too much wine, and the drive had made him tired. He would go to sleep, and then everything would go back to normal.

It was just a bad dream.

* * *

A dozen minutes later, he realized he couldn't fall asleep. Every time he was on the verge of doing so, he opened his eyes, fearing he would see something in the archway.

Yet, every time there was nothing—just the corridor illuminated by the street light.

With a sigh, he turned his back to the corridor.

* * *

Another deep growl made him sweat instantly.

He had his back to the corridor and was facing Mia, who was sleeping.

He wanted to turn, to see what it was, but he was afraid.

What if it's that thing again?

No, he would wait. Maybe he should check if there was an intruder in their room? But that was impossible. He'd locked the door and double-checked it. Plus, the key was in the lock, practically preventing anyone from unlocking it from the outside.

And he'd put the safety latch on. So, no one could enter.

No, it was just in his head.

He would go back to sleep and it would be okay.

* * *

Another deep growl woke him. And now he just *knew* there was someone by the bed.

Yes, someone was by the bed, looking down at him. At his back. He lay there, holding his breath, waiting, looking at Mia. That person was still there, looking at him.

But this is impossible. How could someone be there? I cannot know that! How could I know someone is behind me? This is bullshit. My crazy brain. No, it's all in my imagination.

Slowly, he realized there was no one behind him anymore.

He turned, carefully, building up the courage to look at the opening once more.

There was no one there.

It was a long night. He tossed and turned for a few hours, never managing to get to sleep again, until the sun started filling the world with its light.

Only when it was daylight did he finally drift off.

* * *

"Morning, babe," said Mia, kissing him gently. "Wake up. Today we go up the mountain."

"Ugh, a few more hours, please," said Tibi, moving around in the bed.

"What's wrong? You're usually up by six," said Mia. "Are you sick?"

"No, no," he said, shaking his head. "I had a bad dream. It's nothing, really. But I need a few more hours."

"But then we'll miss the opportunity to drink our coffee at the top of the mountain. Okay, not at the top, but where the cable car drops us."

"Yeah, okay," said Tibi, getting up. "Fine, let's go."

* * *

They reached the cable car station early enough to catch the second cable car. There were two cable cars in rotation, leaving at the same time from one station to the other, meeting halfway. Still, they had to wait a few minutes for their car to arrive, so Tibi and Mia sat on a low concrete wall and watched the incoming people.

"I wonder if they ever sell anything," said Mia, pointing to a relatively old gypsy woman. She wore a long skirt that wrapped around her large waist and skimmed the ground as she walked. It was black with a colorful floral pattern. Her blouse was made from the same fabric and she had a large bandana on her head, again in the same colors.

"Who?" said Tibi, looking around.

"The gypsy. Look, she sells flowers. Who buys flowers when going up the mountain?"

The gypsy woman was holding a large, oval basket under her left arm, packed with a few dozen flower bouquets.

"They are wild flowers, aren't they?" asked Tibi, checking out the woman.

"Yeah. So?"

"You like wild flowers, don't you?"

"I do. But that's not the point. Who buys flowers when going up the mountain? I mean, why is she here so early? Wouldn't people be more likely to buy flowers when coming down the mountain, on their way home?"

"Probably. But maybe she wants to maximize the profit. I don't know. Maybe she has nothing better to do. Wait here."

"What are you doing?" said Mia, yet Tibi was already a few steps away.

13

He reached the gypsy and pointed to her basket. "How much for a bouquet, lady?"

"Oh, my grandson," said the woman in a thick accent, looking around and talking loudly so everyone could hear. "For you, just ten Euros. Here, take it, and may God bring joy to your little lady."

"Oh, ten Euros. That's steep. I can give you one or two maybe," said Tibi, checking her old, wrinkled face. Her skin was dark, now even darker due to constant exposure to the sun, and her smell reminded him of a campfire. A dark mole underneath her left eye caught his attention, yet Tibi tried not to stare at it too much.

"What? Two Euros? No, my grandson, these are quality flowers," continued the old gypsy, still looking around and talking loudly. "The old woman had to climb the mountains to gather all the flowers. She had to bend, pick, then carry back, and then make these beautiful bouquets. Look, my grandson," she said, grabbing one rather small bouquet from her basket and pushing it toward Tibi's nose. "Just smell them, see how nice they—"

She suddenly stopped as she made eye contact with Tibi for the first time. Her mouth was open, as if the last words she had intended to say refused to exit. She slowly lowered the bouquet and then pressed it into Tibi's hand.

"There, my grandson, you have it," she said, now in a faint voice. "Free of charge."

"What? No, that's not what I want," said Tibi, puzzled. "Here, have three Euros," he said, pushing two coins toward the gypsy.

"No, no, you have it. Have it," said the woman, almost dropping the bouquet and then leaving the scene faster than she appeared capable of.

"Aww, are these for me?" said Mia, grabbing the flowers and smelling them. "Mm, I love their perfume. Smells like a field in the summer. See?" she continued, pointing it toward Tibi's nose. But he was looking somewhere behind him. "What's wrong?"

"Nothing… I mean, I don't know," he said, glancing back and forth between Mia and where the gypsy had stood. "Where did she go?"

"I don't know. Why, what happened?"

"It's strange… but never mind," he said, shaking his head. "I'm probably just tired. Never mind that, let's go."

* * *

"You said something about a bad dream?" said Mia as she sipped her large, warm coffee. They were on the terrace of a small restaurant, on top of the mountain.

"It's nothing."

"Come on. Usually people are so eager to tell their dreams. What happened?"

He reluctantly told her what had happened the night before.

"But what do you mean by a shadow?" asked Mia, squinting slightly.

"Say you are outside and it's a dark night. Imagine a car with the lights on, and between you and the car there's a person. Due to the bright light you can only see the shape of the person. You see just a dark shape, like a shadow."

"Yeah, I think I've got it."

"It was the same last night. The streetlight outside sends so much light into that corridor. So the shape I saw was dark. I couldn't make out anything other than a shape."

"It was just a bad dream," said Mia. "You were snoring, and you'd had some alcohol before. Don't worry about it."

"I don't know." He rubbed his chin as he went over the events once more in his mind. "It was so… It felt so real. I've had a few scary dreams right before waking up, but they always disappeared in an instant," said Tibi, snapping his fingers, "right when I woke. But the disturbing thing is, this one didn't. I froze, got stupid scared, then the shadow continued to move. It was horrible. And that sinister feeling afterwards, that someone was by the bed, looking down at me. Urgh. It was really disturbing."

"Poor baby," said Mia, leaning in and kissing him. "Yesterday you didn't exercise. Maybe you need that, to sleep better."

"But I did quite a lot of exercise," he said with a cheeky smile.

She giggled. "You actually did," she added, kissing him again. "But your kick-boxing, maybe you need that."

"Probably. But don't worry about it. It was just a bad dream. It will be fine."

* * *

In the evening they slowly walked back to their room.

"That pie was excellent," said Mia, holding his arm. "Let's stop by the store to get some wine."

"Yeah, good idea," said Tibi, yawning.

"You're tired," said Mia, kissing him. "Poor baby. Come on. We'll go sleep soon."

"I'll take a bath, then I'm done for," he said, kissing her back.

* * *

"How about playing a board game?" asked Tibi later that night, jumping out of bed and going to his duffle bag. "I brought this," he said, pulling out a small wooden box. "We pick some cards, do what is written on each card, and whoever loses the round has to drink a small glass of alcohol."

"Are you trying to get me drunk, mister?" said Mia, smiling with a twinkle in her eyes.

"Maybe," said Tibi, looking around the room.

"Fine. But turn off the lights."

"Let's keep the nightstand lamps on," said Tibi. "We'll need them to read the cards."

* * *

"I'm tired," said Mia, a few hours later. "Where the hell are my pajamas?"

"I think you threw them on the floor," said Tibi, kissing her cheek. "Want me to bring them to you?"

"No, I'm fine. I'll get them."

"And after that we could play another game."

"What? What other game?"

"Well, the same one."

"It's almost 1am. I'm dying. No, let's go to sleep."

"Ugh, fine," said Tibi, getting back into his side of the bed.

"What's wrong?" asked Mia, as she dressed. "Ahh, I know what it is," she said, with a giggle. "You're afraid to go to sleep, aren't you?"

"What? Me? No."

"Ha, ha, yes, you are!"

"Well… okay, fine. I am," said Tibi, smiling but with a hint of shame in his eyes. "Last night was horrible. And that gypsy woman today didn't help. What if I have some sort of a bad mark on me? She saw it with her gypsy eyes. You know how they can read Tarot and tell your fortune by looking at your palm. What if—"

"I thought you didn't believe in that sort of mumbo jumbo," said Mia, getting back into bed.

"I don't. I really don't. Don't laugh. But these last two events were too much of a coincidence."

"I'm telling you, it's nothing. Relax. As you said, it's just a coincidence. Come on. Give me a kiss and let's go to sleep. What, you're still naked? Ha, ha, get dressed."

"Are you sure?" said Tibi, the corner of his mouth turning up into a smile.

"Well, I wouldn't say no, but we're both dead tired. Tomorrow."

* * *

Tibi fell asleep quickly. He was tired from all the walking they'd done that day. Plus, the previous night had taken its toll.

Suddenly, that same growl rang in his head. He opened his eyes, jumping, scared. He thought he saw another shadow behind the thick yellow wall. Only this time it was moving away.

His adrenalin spiked and soon he started feeling hot. Even though the night was cold, the blanket seemed too warm. He was sweating, so he pushed his arms and legs, one at a time, out from under the covers.

Still, he kept sweating.

Why the hell am I so afraid? This is stupid. I'm just having a nightmare. Jesus.

He turned his back on the opening. Still, being mostly out of the blanket now, he felt even more exposed.

He soon turned back, facing the opening once more.

He checked his phone. It was about two dozen minutes past three, just like last time.

Oh, kind of the same time. Is it the same time? I don't remember. Now it's 3:30. What does that mean? Did I wake at 3:20? Next time when it happens, I'll check the phone. Oh, come on, Tibi, stop it. You're being stupid!

He closed his eyes, trying to sleep. Still, just like last night, he couldn't help but open his eyes every few minutes, always fearful he would see something else in the archway.

What if this place is haunted? What if the forest behind us is haunted? I mean, we've all seen Twin Peaks. *What a stupid movie. Why would anyone make such a movie? But it can't be haunted. That would imply Gods exist. Or wouldn't it imply that? I mean, can you have haunted houses and not have religion? Now that I think of it, you can. Damn it.*

Tibi sighed, turning his back on the opening once more.

Say this is a haunted house. Or room. Ah, yes, room! That damn Horza! If he knew this room was haunted, why the hell did he give it to us? What about that reaction he had? Why was he so puzzled by us choosing this room? No, I will go tomorrow and ask to relocate. But what if the whole building is haunted? Could it be? This is horrible. Tibi, come on, think! You don't believe in such things. There are no ghosts. This place cannot be haunted. It's just your imagination.

He looked at Mia, who was sleeping, face up.

I hate sleeping face up, he thought, sighing. *My God, she's beautiful. That idiot Mike is right. How come she's hanging out with me? She could find a taller guy. But I guess we're a good match, if I think of it. But now I'm blowing it! Our first real vacation together and I look like a psychotic wimp. Like an idiot who cannot hold it together.*

He turned around, facing up.

That's it, I'll sleep on my back. Damn, I hate this position. And what was that all about with that damn gypsy? Why the hell did she have to look at me like that? What if I have a mark? I'm marked. We all know how gypsies can put curses on people. They can also remove those curses. But I don't believe in those things. Tibi, you idiot, come on! Relax. You don't believe in such things! The only way for a curse to work is if you believe in it. Otherwise, it doesn't.

Tibi coughed a few times. Suddenly, between coughs, he heard another growl coming from the general direction of the yellow wall. That sound piped through his bones.

What the hell? he thought, looking left instantly.

He saw nothing.

Did I really hear that? Was something there? Jesus Christ, what's wrong with me? He removed the blanket entirely, except for a small portion on his chest.

He turned around, checking his phone again.

3:52. That went fast. Did I fall asleep? Maybe that was it. I coughed in my sleep, and that noise was in my dream. I must go see a doctor. It's not okay to snore too loudly. And I'm rather fit and don't have a cold, so I shouldn't snore like that. But do I snore? Probably, yes, but I bet it's not as loud as to wake me up, dreaming growls and other crazy shit.

He turned his back on the opening again.

To hell with it. It's just a dream. Come on, Tibi. It is just a dream.

Another growl erupted, making his heart jump. He felt a presence behind him, just like the previous night.

He waited it out, and then, just like before, turned around to look.

There was nothing there.

What the hell was that? he yelled in his mind. *What is wrong with me?* He turned to Mia. *Should I wake her? But what if she is just like she was last night, under a spell? Was she under a spell? There are no spells! What the hell, Tibi! Pull yourself together. Relax. Relax!*

He turned back toward the opening, yet he dreaded to look.

Nothing. Of course there's nothing. Let's check the time. Oh, 4:52. I have slept a while since the last growl. This is okay. If I go to sleep now, I'll get a maximum of one more growl before the sun comes up. Gee, nice.

He turned his back on the opening, shifting violently in his bed.

She sleeps through all my movement. It's clear something is wrong. I just know it. Meh, nothing is wrong. God damn it!

He felt his back was exposed and that someone or something had direct access to him, coming from the corridor. He turned once more, face up.

To hell with it. I'll sleep like this. Nothing can happen.

* * *

"Hey, honey, wake up!" said Mia, kissing his jaw and chest gently. "Wake up, babe. Did you sleep well?"

"Mmm," said Tibi, taking a deep breath. "What time is it?"

"It's eight-thirty. We overslept."

"Damn," he said, yawning. "I'm usually up by six-thirty."

"Yeah, well, we were tired. But you still look tired. What's wrong?"

"Oh, nothing. Nothing."

"Did you have that dream again?"

"Ah, no… I mean, yes. I don't want to lie to you. It was creepy. I don't know what the hell is wrong with me."

"Ugh, poor baby," said Mia, hugging him and resting her head on his chest. "Maybe we should take a nap this afternoon. You would feel better."

"Nah, then I wouldn't sleep well at night. No, to hell with it. Let's go. What's the plan for today?"

"We'll take a mountain trail, the one that goes to the top of the mountain. We'll hike, have lunch up there, then return. I want to fix us some sandwiches, so we'll make a quick stop at the store."

* * *

The day progressed well. The hours spent hiking seemed to bring back Tibi's good mood.

"This is great exercise," said Mia, hopping happily. "If I lived here, I would go up the mountain every day."

"Yeah, this is good." Tibi nodded. "I'm not sure about the 'every day' part. I mean, I would get bored after a while."

"True," said Mia. "But think: I could do my daily yoga and fitness training here, instead of in that polluted city of ours."

"As a yoga and fitness trainer, yeah, you could probably find work here. But for the tourists only. And I think you'd have to come up with a special program for them. No one would come to the mountains and go to normal yoga or fitness classes. They would rather take a hike up the mountain. Still, maybe you could come up with something like 'All new yoga practice to take advantage of the healthy negative ions'," he said, moving his hands around as if he was showcasing a logo. "Or, better yet, 'Amazing stretching techniques for improving your hikes'."

"Oh, you are so good at coming up with captions," said Mia, giggling.

"Pfft. We can improve on that, of course. But that's for you. Me, on the other hand… I'm a game designer, working for a big company. We have no studio here, and I have to be in the office. I wish there was a way for us to work remotely, but I don't think that will ever happen. Not in my lifetime."

"I know, I know," said Mia, grabbing his hand as they walked. "I was just daydreaming."

"Yeah, I know," said Tibi, kissing her. "And who knows, maybe someday we'll get a chance to do that. We're still young."

* * *

Evening came and they were back in their room.

"Let's play a board game," said Tibi.

"Ugh, I'm beat. And so are you," said Mia, yawning. "I don't feel like it."

"Maybe we can watch a movie?"

"Fine. What's on?"

"I don't know. Let me check."

They found a Michael Dudikoff action movie and they enjoyed it for about an hour and a half.

"I'm dead. I'll go to sleep."

"No, wait, let's play—"

"Babe, come on. It's midnight. Go to sleep. Please," said Mia, followed by a long yawn. "We'll play tomorrow, I promise."

They kissed, and Tibi turned off the light.

He threw a quick glance at the opening. The light was still pouring into the corridor and he got the impression a shadow would appear at any moment.

Yet, he was very tired, and it was so difficult to stay awake.

* * *

A growl rang in his ears and he opened his eyes. He had his back to the opening, so all he saw was Mia sleeping next to him.

To hell with it, he thought, and he started to turn. *What will I see? Is it a shadow? So what if it's a shadow?*

As he finished turning, he caught a glimpse of what looked like a hand moving away.

Oh no! What the hell was that? That was a hand!

He shook his head.

"That's it," he said out loud, and got out of bed. He checked his phone. It was 3:22. He got up, took two steps and reached the opening, where the light switches were.

He turned on the light inside the room, yet he didn't have the courage to look into the corridor.

"What is it, babe?" said Mia, mumbling.

"Nothing. Go back to sleep," he said, getting back under the comforter and kissing her temple.

"What's with the mmmmm mm."

"What? You mean the lights?"

"Yeah."

"Never mind that. Go to sleep."

* * *

"Let's go home," said Tibi, early in the morning, his face etched with fatigue.

"What?" said Mia, blinking as she tried to adjust to the light in the room. "What happened? And why are the lights on?"

"I couldn't sleep. I heard those growls every few hours throughout the night. The first one was at 3:22, and I think every night it's happened around the same time."

"Really? Why?"

"I don't know. I have no idea what 3:22 means."

"What time it is now?"

"It's five-thirty."

"And you want to go home?"

"Maybe we can go to the seaside. It's Wednesday already, and we were supposed to go there on Sunday, right? So maybe we can go four days earlier. Can you call them?"

"Yeah, okay," said Mia after a moment's hesitation. "You wanna go now?"

"If you're okay with it. We can beat the traffic."

"Okay, fine," said Mia, getting out of bed and resting a bit on the edge. "I'll take a quick shower, get dressed and then we can go."

* * *

"Ready?" said Mia with a halfhearted smile, unlocking the room door.

"Yeah," said Tibi, emerging from the bathroom and looking at its door. "Let's leave this door open, like it was when we came," he said, going over to the bed, grabbing his duffle bag and throwing one last glance around the room. "I think we packed everything."

As he entered the corridor and moved toward the room's main door, he suddenly felt a pressure in his head.

"Ah," he said, touching his forehead with his free left hand.

"What's wrong?"

"Just a headache. Must be the lack of sleep. Come on."

Mia exited, and Tibi turned around to close the door.

As he pulled the handle, the door felt difficult to close, like a draft was blowing inside the room, exerting an opposing force.

"Jesus," mumbled Tibi, pulling vigorously. At the same time, a gust of wind made the bathroom door slam shut.

"Wow, what a strong draft," said Mia. "You should have closed that door."

"Yeah, I should have," said Tibi with a huff as he finally managed to close the main door. "But that was really strange," he added as they headed down the stairs.

"What was?"

"The draft was blowing inside from the hallway. So it was difficult to close the room door."

"And?"

"While the bathroom door closed toward the corridor."

"Ah."

"Yeah. So the two drafts were both pushing toward the corridor."

"You're starting to get me scared now," said Mia, chuckling. "I bet there's a logical explanation for that."

"Yeah, probably. Hi there," said Tibi, upon seeing Emi at the reception desk. "We have to go. Thank you for having us."

"But, but… is there something wrong?" he asked, his brow furrowed.

"No, nothing. Everything is fine. We just have to go. Something came up."

"But you paid until Sunday, right? I mean, I don't think I can refund you. I'll have to talk to—"

"Not to worry," said Tibi. "We're fine. See you!"

"Bye! Oh, just a sec. Did you take anything from the minibar?"

"Nope," said Tibi.

"Ah, yes," said Mia, grabbing something from her pocket. "I took a water bottle, for the road."

"Ah," said Emi, pausing for a few seconds. "Nah, don't worry about it," he added, waving. "Have a safe trip."

"Bye," they both said, and left.

"Why didn't you try to get a refund?" asked Mia on their way to the car.

"I didn't want to tell them why I want to leave. Then they would probably have tried to give me another room, and, you know, I didn't want to look like an idiot."

"Yeah, I get it, but you could have just given them a random reason for leaving early. You're not an idiot if you try to get your money back."

"Yeah, I know, true. I think I just wanted to get out of there as soon as possible. Especially after the whole draft thing."

"*That* was strange."

"This whole place is giving me the creeps," he added, throwing the luggage into the trunk while looking up at the Three Bears guesthouse.

2 SEASIDE

"Hello. I'm calling about a reservation. We booked a room, starting this Sunday… No, no. We want to extend it. Yes. We'd like to come sooner. When? Ah, today would be awesome. Oh… When? Friday?" Mia turned her blue eyes toward Tibi, who nodded. "Yeah, Friday will do. We'll be there."

"So, Friday is it?" said Tibi.

"Yeah. We can try to find something else for today and tomorrow, in the same resort, you know? And then switch places."

"No, I'm fine, I guess. We could stay a couple of days back in the city."

"But I don't want to feel like vacation is over," said Mia with a sigh, her brows drawn together.

"Yeah, I know what you mean. And, look, I'm sorry. I don't know what happened. I don't believe in these things, haunted houses or spirits or ghosts or whatever that was. Yet those events were so… disturbing."

"Yeah, I understand. Don't worry, babe, we'll be fine. You'll get some sleep, and tomorrow you'll be as good as new."

"Yeah, but I don't want you to feel like vacation is over either. We should stay together."

"I can come to your apartment. I don't have to go home. And my folks still think I am away, so no harm there."

"Ugh, but my parents are in town. They wanted to see my brother, so now he's sleeping in my room, while I'm gone. It would be too crowded; the apartment is rather small."

"Ah, okay. Then come to my place. We've done it before. It will still feel like a vacation. And the next couple of days we can go out to exercise and play hot-seat *Heroes*."

"Okay, that sounds awesome," said Tibi, smiling. "I still don't understand your father. Does he really think we just hold hands and exchange innocent kisses?"

"Come on, don't be mean," said Mia, giggling. "He's old fashioned. You'll sleep in my room and I'll sleep in the living room, as usual."

"Yeah, yeah, I know," said Tibi, continuing to smile.

"My mother knows what's going on, naturally. My dad is a bit off in his own world."

* * *

"Hello, Ms. Stoian. Hello, sir," said Tibi, entering the small hallway of the apartment.

"Hi, Tibi, how are you?" said a plump lady, moving busily around, picking up some objects and stuffing them in a drawer. "How was your trip? Mia tells me there were some issues with—"

"Mom," said Mia.

"Yes, yes, I mean, I'm happy you guys are here."

"How about a whiskey, son?" asked Mr. Stoian, appearing from the living room. He seemed about ten years older than his wife and, unlike Mia, was fairly short, although very wide.

"Thank you, sir. Yes, don't mind if I do."

"How was your trip to the mountains? What happened?"

"Ah, don't worry about that," said Ms. Stoian. "Come, Tibi, go drop off your backpack. Do you guys want something to eat?"

"Yeah, Mom, we're hungry. But I hope it's vegetarian," said Mia. "I have to take some things from my room, and then I will be out of your way," she said, this time to Tibi, treating him to a seductive smile.

"Ah, yes," said Tibi, louder than usual. "Please do," he then added in his normal voice, feeling a bit awkward about being loud before.

Mia went to her room, and Tibi followed. She took a last sip from the plastic water bottle as Tibi drew her into his arms.

"Stop it," she whispered as he kissed her neck, his hands roaming over her body.

"Let's do it right now, Miss Stoian," said Tibi, turning her around to kiss her lips.

"No. Jesus. You're crazy," said Mia, grinning. "I have to move out now or they will get suspicious."

She rearranged her blouse, then went ahead and opened her armoire, grabbing some clothes.

"How much do you think this costs?" said Tibi, picking up and checking the water bottle.

"What?"

"The bottle. You know, the one that Emi gave us for free."

"Ah. It's probably overpriced at the guesthouse. But I guess it's less than half a Euro if you buy in bulk. Why?"

"Just wondering how much he gave us. You know, at the end. 'Don't worry about it'," he added, moving his hand while faking the tone of a rich snob. "Keep the water. Pfft. And they gave us a haunted room."

She chuckled. "I guess. Well, it's good we put all that behind us," she said, grabbing the bottle from him and throwing it into the bin a few steps away. "I've got my stuff. If you want to go to the gym, you can join me. I could use some exercise."

"Yeah, let's go."

* * *

Evening came, and as the movie ended everyone went to bed.

"Goodnight, Tibi," said Mia loudly as her parents exited the living room. She climbed onto the sofa bed and pulled up a blanket.

"Goodnight," said Tibi, also at a high volume. "Well, well, well," he then added, in a quiet voice, once they heard the parents' door close. "What do we have here?" he continued, his hands sliding below the blanket.

"Ha, no, go away," whispered Mia, smiling.

"I will, but not this instant."

"Come on, my dad is crazy. He'll go ballistics if he finds you here."

"But I'll be quick about it."

"Yeah, how could anyone refuse such a tempting offer?" Mia giggled. "Come on. In two days, we'll be at the seaside. We can do whatever we like there."

"Okay, okay," said Tibi, kissing her again. "I'll go. But I'll remember that," he added, faking an accent.

"Ha! I hope so."

Tibi left the room, closed the door, then walked down the corridor and entered Mia's room, now his for the night.

He changed into his pajamas and slid between the fresh bed sheets. As he browsed a bit on his phone, he couldn't shake the feeling that something was off. He looked around a few times, yet he couldn't work out what it was.

"Eh," he said out loud, putting down the phone and turning off the light. "Time to sleep."

* * *

He sensed a presence. Someone or something was there, in that room. He couldn't quite say what it was, but it was there. He opened his eyes and looked toward his feet. He could see the armoire and, next to it, the door. On the left-hand side of the room was a desk and a chair. To the right was the wall, and the bed was pushed against it.

There was a large window behind the headboard, and some light was coming into the room, enough for him to see everything properly.

There was nothing there, yet he could still feel that presence.

Tibi turned around, with his back against the wall, and watched the desk.

Come on, not again, he thought. *Why is this happening to me? At least there are no creepy shadows moving around. Come on, Tibi, think of something nice. Mia in a bathing suit, a few days from now. Yes, that.*

He tried to relax and think positive thoughts.

Still, something was bothering him.

Tibi moved around, changing position: left, right, even face up.

But that presence wouldn't go away.

* * *

Morning found him more exhausted than ever.

"I've got to go home," said Tibi, yawning. "You know, I realized I want to see my parents. I haven't seen them in months, and since they're in the city, why not? I can bunk up with my brother, in my room, and I'll come back to pick you up tomorrow."

"What? Why?" asked Mia. "Is there something wrong?"

"No, no, nothing's wrong," said Tibi. "It just occurred to me."

"But I thought you wanted us to spend this time together."

"I still want that. It's just, you know, half a day really."

"I see," said Mia. "I'm sorry you… I don't know what I could—"

"No, no. Really. You're amazing. Yeah, don't laugh, but it's not you, it's me. I said don't laugh," said Tibi, with a chuff of laughter. "I'll just go home for a bit and come back tomorrow."

"Okay, fine. I get it, yeah," said Mia, sighing. "When do you leave?"

"Right now. I'll call you later."

* * *

"So, that's the story," said Tibi, using the hands-free as he was driving. "That's what happened, so that's why we're back from the mountain resort. And I think something followed me back to the city."

"This is so strange," said Mike over the car's speakers. "I mean, you always struck me as a sissy, you know, but this takes the biscuit."

"Ha, ha, yeah, I always knew I could count on your support."

Mike laughed. "But, seriously, have you had enough broccoli? Maybe that's the issue right there." Mike let out another bark of laughter.

"Jesus. Come on, Mike. Help me out here. What the hell is wrong with me? Is it something I did? Am I strange? I mean, I'm a Christian by birth, but I'm not a believer, so is this some sort of punishment? Am I doing something wrong? What is it?"

"I'm an atheist, too, if that makes you happy," said Mike. "You should be a true Christian, though, and a practicing one. You know, try to save your soul from being some sort of herbivore. Okay, okay, I'll stop. Sorry," said Mike, while they both laughed. "The whole door incident and gust of wind that happened right before you left? I'm no expert, but say something really was there. How come it followed you? I mean, why you? Will it follow you further? Is it with you in your car right now?"

"No. I mean, I hope not. But I don't feel any presence here. You know? While there, in Mia's room, I felt it."

"I see. Besides your things, did you take anything from that room back to the city?"

"Yeah."

"You did? What?"

"I stole the towels and a pillow."

"Ha, ha."

"Come on. I didn't take anything, of course."

"Hey, I'm just asking. I mean, if you need some money, just let me know."

"Yeah, yeah. So, no, nothing."

"Ah! Could it be linked to the room number?" asked Mike.

"How come?"

"You know, twenty-six is two times thirteen. Now that's a hint and a half."

"That's stupid."

"There were two of you, so a thirteen each. Thirteen is bad… No, it's stupid, you're right. Okay, let me think. Did you take a picture of the interior?"

"Umm… no. Why?"

"Maybe something got linked into the picture."

"How the hell could that happen?"

"Hey, I said I'm no expert. I don't know anything about poltergeists or ghosts or spirits or souls or whatever it is. I'm just throwing ideas around."

"Okay, okay, sorry. No, I didn't take a picture."

"Because, you know… you take a picture and somehow that thing gets *linked* to your phone or whatever."

"Yeah, yeah, got it. No, I didn't. And I'm starting to feel cheated now. I should have asked for some kind of refund. I mean, what the hell? And I'm annoyed how that guy *gave* us that water bottle as a gift. Like some lord throwing the help a bone."

"What water bottle?"

Tibi paused for a few seconds.

"You'll think I'm an idiot. But I'm driving, so I can't focus that much. Yes, we did take something from that room. But it was just a plastic bottle. We drank the water and threw it in the bin in Mia's room."

"And if we are to assume there is some connection, that means that whatever was there followed you here because of that plastic bottle."

"Right."

"So now it's just a matter of finding out if throwing away the bottle will fix the problem. Or will that thing linger on? For example, attached to the room."

"Jesus. I can't believe I'm talking about such nonsense."

"How is Mia handling all this? Did she finally realize she's way out of your league and dump you already?"

"She's rather supportive, I guess. I mean, she came back home with me and didn't complain about it at all. I didn't have the courage to tell her about last night though. I'm starting to feel like a wimp."

"You should have considered that when you told her you don't eat meat."

"I was wondering when you'd bring that up again. And you know she's vegetarian as well."

"That's fine. She's a woman. You're a man. You're supposed to eat things that eat the things she eats."

"Yeah, well. I'm lucky I found her."

"That I agree with."

"Ha, ha."

"Anyway," said Mike, "I have the boss throwing me glances. I have to go. Stay strong and let me know how things go tonight. If you're still haunted, don't come to me. I don't want your shitty restless souls ruining *my* sleep. I have *World of Warcraft* for that."

"Yeah, you're safe. I would choose a haunted house over sharing an apartment with you again."

"Those were the days," said Mike in a melancholic tone.

"Yeah, and we were students. Now, go. I don't want you to lose your job. You might be forced to start eating leafy greens and lose a few hundred pounds because of it."

"Ha, ha, ha. Okay, man, see ya. Take care."

Tibi pulled into the parking lot, parked and got out, now completely exhausted.

* * *

"Hey, babe," said Mia over the phone that evening. "How are you?"

"I'm fine," said Tibi, before pausing to yawn. "I'm so tired though. I'll go to sleep soon."

"Say hi to your folks."

"I will, thank you. Oh, and tell your mother I'm sorry I left without saying goodbye. I didn't mean to seem like I ran away."

"She was out anyway. They were both out. It's Thursday; they had left for work."

"Ah… so we were all alone in the house?"

"Yeah, you dufus."

"Damn. Why didn't you say anything?"

"You seemed so eager to go."

"Yeah… Sorry about that. It was… it was strange. Look, I'll tell you. I think something followed us from the guesthouse. I felt a presence in the room last night. I slept badly because I sensed something there."

"What? Why didn't you say anything?"

"I… I didn't want to look like an idiot."

"Just a sec. Wait," said Mia, putting down the phone. "Don't hang up!" Her last sentence came through the phone from afar, yet Tibi heard it.

Seconds passed, and Tibi continued to hold the phone to his ear, looking braindead at some stupid show on TV while waiting for Mia. She returned about two minutes later. "There. You were saying?"

"You did that on purpose, right? You want to tape me saying it?" Tibi forced a chuckle.

"No, no. I talked to Mom."

"So, I was saying that I don't want to look like an idiot. Truth is, I care what you think about me."

"Ah, that's sweet," said Mia. "I care what you think about me too."

"What did you talk about with your mother?"

"Ah. I told her about the presence, that you think something followed us. She'll handle it."

"Wow. Really? How?"

"That's why you should have told me in the morning. She'll take care of it. Don't worry about it."

"Oh, and you have to throw the bottle away."

"What bottle?"

"The plastic bottle, the one we took from the room. Mike's theory is that the thing followed us from the guesthouse to your place by using that bottle as a vehicle."

"Okay. I'll tell her about the bottle as well," said Mia. The sound of her voice made Tibi think she was smiling.

"Fine. So, I guess I'll go to sleep."

"Great. Sleep well! Love you."

"Ha!" said Tibi, grinning.

"Ah. Damn!"

"You said it first!"

"It was just a reflex! It doesn't count," said Mia, trying to hold in a giggle.

"Well, there's clearly some truth in it. And you said it first. So, yeah, I should add that I might love you too."

"Might?"

"Okay, fine. I love you too. I'm just sorry we said it over the phone. But I'll make it up to you."

"You'd better!"

* * *

Next morning, Tibi was downstairs, in front of the apartment building, waiting for Mia to come out and resume their vacation.

They went to spend a happy week at the seaside.

The following Saturday, the car pulled up, letting out two very bronzed lovers. Tibi and Mia went up the stairs to her apartment and rang the bell.

"Good day, Mr. and Ms. Stoian," said Tibi, dropping off Mia's duffle bag.

"Hello children," said Mia's mother, smiling at them. "How was your vacation?"

"We had a great time, Mother," said Mia. "Tibi will spend the night here and go home tomorrow."

"Yeah, if that's okay with you," said Tibi. "My parents and my brother leave tomorrow, so it's a bit crowded there still tonight. I'll leave early in the morning to meet them, but I'd rather spend the night here. Sleeping next to my brother in that small bed was not such a good idea last time."

"No problem, no problem at all. Are you children hungry?"

* * *

"Ugh," said Tibi that evening, as he was about to leave the living room to go into the bedroom. "I'm ashamed to admit it, but I'm a bit scared to go to bed."

"Ah, don't worry," said Mia, who was tucked into the sofa bed, Tibi kneeling next to her. "I talked to Mom. She solved it."

"Really? What did she do?"

"She called a priest. We have a good family friend who's a priest at a church nearby. He came and performed a ritual in the room. You know, to cleanse it, to cast away the bad things and restless spirits. Basically, blessing the room. Oh, and the plastic bottle is long gone."

"Oh, wow," said Tibi, raising a skeptical eyebrow. "I didn't used to believe in these things, but that sounds great, I guess. Goodnight, my love."

"Goodnight, babe," said Mia, kissing Tibi.

He went into Mia's room and slept like a baby.

3 THREE YEARS LATER

Mike entered the open-plan office, dropped his backpack on the floor and sat on the chair with a loud huff.

"Man, I'm beat," he said.

"How come?" asked Tibi, who was typing something at his computer.

"I didn't sleep last night. I played some *WOW*. At some point we decided to enter another raid and it took, like, forever to finish it."

"That's why I don't play games."

"That's smart. Especially being a game designer. You know, you're trying to keep an unbiased eye on things. All your designs are original and never overlap—"

"Yeah, yeah, laugh all you want. I don't play games that need two lifetimes to complete. But I do play some games, and I check reviews. So, yeah, I'm up to date with the industry."

"Fine, fine," said Mike. He yawned. "What the hell are you doing with all that time at home by yourself?"

"What, you mean the evenings?"

"Yeah."

"You know, making sweet love to Mia."

"Okay, and after those ten minutes?"

"You mean after those four hours."

"Yeah, right," said Mike, laughing.

"I don't know. Besides going to the gym, we just stay in and watch movies. We play with the dog and the cats."

"I still don't understand how you convinced that wonderful creature to take you as her husband. When was that, two years ago?"

"Two years ago today, in fact."

"No, really?" said Mike, faking surprise while he leaned toward his backpack.

"Yeah. Why? What's going on?"

"Nothing," said Mike, grabbing something from his bag and throwing it toward Tibi. "Happy celebration, or whatever you say on these occasions."

Tibi caught a small package, poorly wrapped. "What is this? What the hell, you didn't have to."

"No worries. I mean, I'm surprised that, two years later, she still comes home to you, you being a vegan and all."

Tibi snickered. "First, I'm not a vegan, I'm a vegetarian, and you know that."

Mike scoffed.

"Second, I told you, she can't get enough of this."

"Enough of what? Having a husband shorter than her?"

"Ha, ha, come on, stop it. I know all the jokes. Now, let me open this thing," said Tibi, ripping the paper and exposing a cheap, gray cardboard box. He opened it. "Oh, wow. A watch?"

"Yeah. I know you're a fan."

Tibi was laughing violently.

"What is it?" said a colleague two desks over.

"Man. You know me all too well," said Tibi, wiping a tear after all that laughter. "Yeah. I love it. Thank you."

"No, really, what is it?" continued the colleague.

"Well, he knows I love high-end wristwatches. Of course, I can't afford one. But, you know, I like to read the reviews on the Internet, look at the pictures, videos, all that."

"And?"

"And he gave me one of those cheap-ass replicas where you can buy five for three Euros or something," continued Tibi, laughing some more. "I will keep it. I swear."

"Nice," said Mike, smiling happily. "Oh, but don't throw away the… no, that, the wrapping. Yeah, there's something more."

36

Tibi looked at the wrapping and found a small envelope, the size of the box of the cheap watch. "What is it?" he said, opening it and pulling out two tickets. "Wow! Tickets to the match? The one we play tomorrow against France?"

"Yup," said Mike, with a wide smile.

"Wow. This is awesome. I tried to get some, but it was sold out. We'll go together, right?"

"I can join, of course. But in case Mia would like to go, I completely understand. You know, so it can be a gift for both of you."

"No, don't worry. Mia is not into this, and she'll be happy for me. Man, this might be better than the watch."

"Hey," said Mike, faking seriousness, "that's an original Relex!"

* * *

"We have great seats," said Tibi, loudly, as the stadium was packed.

"Yeah, you can smell the players' sweat from here," said Mike, pulling out a partially flattened plastic bottle. "Vodka?"

"No, really?" asked Tibi. "How the hell did you get that in?"

"The guy checking me did a very poor job. What can I say. So?"

"Yeah, of course, let me have it."

"Good, isn't it?" said Mike, retrieving the bottle. "That's the good stuff. My grandfather's own recipe."

"Whew, yeah. Strong one. If we drink all this, I'll get drunk."

"Ha! Here's to you and to a happy marriage!" Mike took a big gulp.

"Thanks, man," said Tibi, tapping his back.

A few minutes passed as they watched the players enter the field and then start running, stretching and warming-up.

"You know," said Tibi, all of a sudden, in a serious tone. "I'm still having that dream."

Mike's smile evaporated as he looked out over the field. "Oh. Man. How often?"

"Once or twice a week… at least."

"Is it the same?"

Tibi cleared his throat. "Always the same. Down to the sounds,

37

smells… I don't know what's happening."

"You're still alone, in the woods?"

"In the woods, yes. And I'm looking for something. I know it's there, but it's not there, you know? And I look and I look. And eventually I find a large pile of building material scraps, and then I hear the growl. The one from that damn room, you know? At that point, I wake up. Every time."

"That *is* strange. Have you tried getting some professional help?"

"Like what?"

"I mean, the good thing is you've already come to terms with having a micro penis, you know, from all those plants you eat—"

"You fat bastard," said Tibi, trying to control himself, but letting out a stifled laugh.

"—yet you could still go see a shrink, you know, for this other thing," continued Mike, a bit more seriously. "No, but really. What does Mia say about this?"

"She's concerned. I mean, she didn't experience any of the stuff that happened to me. Initially I tried to tone it down, but over the years I've told her everything. And you know how she's religious and stuff."

"Yeah. A strange combination, indeed."

"Yeah, but that's not what I meant. She's a believer. I mean, okay, she doesn't go to church weekly, and she doesn't like all those priests and how they expect money for everything they do. Yet, she believes in God and she thinks Jesus is always with you, no matter where you are. That is, if you're a good person, of course."

"Yeah, you told me."

"Right," said Tibi, grabbing the bottle from Mike's hand, just as the players were moving off the field to prepare for the start of the match. "And she really believes that something is there. You know, some lost soul, left behind, that somehow connected to me."

"And you believe that?"

"No. I mean, I don't believe in those things. I always scoffed when reading about them. But remember that time when I couldn't sleep in her bedroom?"

"Yeah, well, I can imagine why," said Mike, trying to hold in his laughter.

"You're sick, you know that, right? No, but really. Her mother called some local priest from some small church. He did something there, you know, some sermon of some sort, and then I've never had issues sleeping there since. Never! And I don't think it's just in my head. I'm starting to think Mia is right."

"This is something you'll hear yourself saying a lot more, now that you're married. I mean, it's been two years already… I hear now is when things get real."

"Ha. Yeah, well. And I think I know what I'll do."

"Don't tell me. You finally decided to put that beard of yours to good use?"

"What do you mean?"

"It's obvious. You want to become a priest, don't you?" said Mike, grinning.

"No," said Tibi, throwing a quick smile. "I'm thinking about going back."

"Back? Back where? To that room?"

"Yeah. To Room 26. Go there and investigate. But this time, I'll be open to solving the problem."

"But why? I mean… why would you go there? You have a good life, you have a hot wife. You should spend your time making babies, not indulging some bad dreams."

"There might be more than just—"

"More, okay. But these things are just that: dreams."

"There's also what happened three years ago, which puzzles me."

"Don't stress about it. Why do you keep obsessing over it?"

"True. But besides that, I have these strange dreams every few nights. And the strange thing is, they happen at the same exact time. I mean, I have strong mental health, I think—"

"Well, not judging by the food you eat."

"—but I'm starting to feel pressure. You know? I need to put this one to bed. Pun intended."

"You said these dreams happen at the same time?"

"Yeah. 3:22," said Tibi, taking another sip from the plastic bottle.

"I see. Have you thought about waking up at 3:20 and looking around to see what happens?"

"Yes, of course I did. I tried that last year. Man, this vodka is strong. I'll go to bed drunk."

"And what happened?"

"Nothing happened. I woke up for two weeks in a row, day by day. Alarm set at 3:19. I looked around our bedroom: nothing. The only good thing was I didn't have the dreams anymore, since I was already awake."

"Strange. And what was Mia doing?"

"She slept through it every time. The alarm didn't wake her, and I didn't want to upset her with my silly experiments."

"I see… Ah, they're coming in," said Mike, standing up and applauding. "Let's show those Frenchies what we're capable of!"

* * *

"How was the game, babe?" said Mia, kissing Tibi as he entered their apartment. "Ah, you've been drinking."

"Yeah. Mike had some homemade vodka. It was awesome."

"How is Mike?"

"Same old. Still pulling my leg about being vegetarian. I like him."

"I baked cheese pie. Want some?"

"Wow, nice. Yes, please. My stomach aches after all that vodka. And I need tons of water."

They entered the kitchen and Tibi gulped a glass of water.

"Phew. That's better. Oh, I also told Mike about my idea."

"Which idea? About Room 26?"

"Yeah. I just don't know when to go."

"Well, why don't you just decide?"

"What, now?"

"Yeah," said Mia, putting a plate on the table. "I mean, you can call the guesthouse. Just book Room 26 and that's it. Let's go this weekend. And if it's full, we'll go the following week. I'll go with you; I can have someone replace me at the gym for a few days."

"For me it's a bit more complicated than that, but I can try to take a few days off if the weekend doesn't work. Hmm, this is good pie. Scrumptious!"

"My mother's secret recipe."

"Ugh," said Tibi, simulating a disgusted face.

"Stop it," said Mia, and Tibi grabbed and kissed her.

"You know," he said in a charming tone, "I told Mike how we spend like four hours a day making love."

"Mm," answered Mia in a similar tone, "do you often lie to your friends?"

"Well, let's try and see, shall we?"

* * *

He opened his eyes. He was in a forest. It was evening, and dark clouds were massing, covering the stars. A strong wind was blowing and the rustling of leaves and tree branches was loud.

He had very little time to find it. But it was there, somewhere.

He started moving, heading deeper into the forest, climbing the side of the mountain. It got darker, and the leaves struck his body as the wind intensified.

He suspected, no, he knew something was following him. Something was watching him as he advanced, yet he felt safe. He pressed on.

The forest was not so dense now. Suddenly, he could see a clearing through the branches crisscrossing in front of him. He picked up the pace and soon found himself in a small, fifty-foot-wide opening inside the forest.

A lot of building materials were there, and something was underneath that pile. He knew it.

He suddenly realized he was carrying a shovel. He took it and pushed away some of the scraps. He kept digging as a flash lit the dark forest. A few seconds later, thunder struck.

He suddenly hit something hard, making his arms shake, just as the first drops of rain fell upon his head.

He woke up, sweaty.

"Ugh, poor baby," said Mia, kissing him gently. "Again?"

"Yeah." Tibi sighed.

"Come on, call them. You need to fix this. Look," she said, indicating the desk clock, it's past three."

"It's 3:22, to be exact," said Tibi, turning his face toward her.

"Ha! It says 3:23."

"That desk clock is not synchronized to the second. Check the phone. That one should be really close to earth clock."

"You're right," said Mia, grabbing and checking her phone. "Wow. Call them first thing in the morning. You cannot go on like this."

"Yeah," said Tibi, getting out of the bed. "Or, better yet, I'll call now, maybe someone's at the desk."

He reached the living room and sat on a chair, leaning his left elbow on the table.

"Hello? Yeah, hello. I want to make an appoint… ah, to book a room. Yes. Yes. Ah, starting Friday, until Sunday. Oh, it's all booked? Damn. How about starting Sunday?"

"I can't Sunday," whispered Mia, who was next to him. "I have to be at the gym. Try Monday."

"Sorry, how about starting Monday? Yeah. Yes, with my wife. Yes, can I choose the room? Oh… but I want a specific one, Emi. Yeah, I know you. Yes, we've met. I stayed there about three years ago. I want… Yes. Yes, and we were in Room 26, and I loved it. I want the same— Yeah, I know. Okay, see what you can do. I really want that room. Here, I'll tell you my phone number. Call me anytime."

Tibi put down his phone, kissed Mia, and went to grab another glass of water.

* * *

The phone rang loudly in the office.

"Hey, mister designer, can you please pick it up?" said Mike, rubbing his forehead. "You're waking everybody up."

"Yeah, yeah, sorry," said Tibi, answering the call. "Yes? Oh, hi, Emi. Yeah. Oh… that's bad. Oh, is it right underneath it? Okay, got it. Fine, okay. We'll be there. Yes. Thank you."

"What was that all about?" asked Mike.

"I'm going back to that guesthouse. They don't have the same room, so they gave me Room 16. Right underneath it."

"What? Why?"

"What do you mean why? Why what? Why am I going back? I just told you yesterday."

"Yeah, you did. But I hoped it was just a phase."

"No. I mean, I have to take care of it. I had the dream again last night."

"You're a nut job, I get it. But… I mean…"

"What are you afraid of?" asked Tibi. "You think we'll give you our pets to babysit while we're gone?" he asked, grinning.

"Stop it. I know your brother does that."

"Then what is it? I didn't know you believed in these things."

Mike shook his head. "I don't. But seeing you like this… I'm worried about you. I mean, what if?"

"Yeah. I know what you mean," said Tibi in a quieter voice.

* * *

They pulled into the Three Bears' parking lot. It was a beautiful Monday afternoon.

Tibi and Mia went up the stairs and into the dark-brown guesthouse.

"Hey, Emi," said Tibi, smiling briefly at the receptionist. "How come you're here all the time?"

"What do you mean, Mr. Coman?" asked Emi, smiling at Tibi and Mia.

"I mean, last time we were here we left at six in the morning and you were at your desk. I called you a few days ago, at four am, and you answered. Then you called me at the office, and it was about eleven. Now you're here, and it's five pm."

"Ah, that. Well, due to attempts at cost reduction, I'm the only one on the job. I don't need too much sleep, and when I do, I sleep in a room back here during the night, so I can be on call twenty-four hours a day."

"So, I woke you?"

"Yes. But not to worry; it's my job."

"Wow, okay. I see. Well, see you later then. We know our way to the room."

"See you, sir. Enjoy your stay."

* * *

"Man, it's three years later, but that Emi looks the same, very

43

young," said Mia, sitting on the bed. "Early thirties at most. It's difficult to tell his age."

"I guess," said Tibi, grabbing his backpack and opening it. "But he keeps on dressing like my grandparents."

"I feel sorry for him."

"Why? His voice?"

"Yeah."

"Don't be. That's life and there's nothing you can do about it. Ah, this little hedgehog will be just fine," said Tibi, grabbing a small cube from his backpack. "Unfortunately, we're in the wrong room."

"What is that?" asked Mia.

"A camera. It has a built-in accumulator and memory, so it can record twenty hours or so, all autonomously."

"You're going to record here anyway, even if it's not *the* room?"

"I don't think there's anything to record," he said, pushing some buttons on the little black plastic box, "but since I have it, I'll set it up."

"Great," said Mia, shaking her head. "Just what I wanted: to be filmed while I sleep. Can anyone get ahold of these recordings?"

"Only if I sell them," said Tibi, grinning. "Come, give me a kiss."

"I hope it's turned off," said Mia.

"I can turn it on if you want."

"Pfft."

* * *

"Let's go eat," said Mia.

They were in bed, and the room was messy. Their backpacks were on the floor and the bedspread was thrown in a corner.

"I have to tidy up first," said Tibi, getting up after briefly kissing his wife.

"Come on," said Mia, grabbing her clothes. "The sky's not going to fall if this room is not sparkling while we're out."

"Just a few things," said Tibi, grabbing the bedspread.

* * *

"I'm tired," said Mia, yawning as she lay in bed. "What time is it? Oh, it's eleven already."

"Yeah, me too," said Tibi. "That food was awesome, but I'm beat. Goodnight."

"Goodnight, babe."

The room was almost identical to Room 26, the one above. Almost identical, except the colors. This one was yellow all over, and the bathroom tiles were a different color as well.

Tibi turned to his left, looking toward the archway. He could see a few other small differences. The top of the walls in this room had a painted motif, and the one separating the room from the corridor was thinner.

Yet the light was still coming in through a narrow window, just like the one on the second floor.

Those lights are creepy. When we build our dream house, I will not have these kind of—

"Honey?"

"Yes?" said Tibi, startled.

"Have you turned on the camera?"

"Oh! Right. Damn. Sorry, I was so tired."

"Nothing to apologize about. I mean, I'll count this as another failure, of course," said Mia, giggling.

"Yes, yes," said Tibi, rising. "Where the hell is that bathrobe? It's cold out here."

"Mm, it's soooo good in bed," said Mia, slowly moving underneath her warm comforter.

"I'll come back soon," said Tibi. He pressed a few buttons on the camera, which made a short beep. "There. It's on. I'll point it at the opening. It will capture whatever happens in the hallway."

"Come back to bed," said Mia, already half asleep.

* * *

Thud.

Tibi opened his eyes.

Thud.

Silence.

He was leaning left, toward the opening. A flash of cold sweat ran down his back as his eyes moved around, trying to catch a glimpse of whatever was happening in the hallway.

Still, nothing was there.

Tibi turned right to see Mia sleeping peacefully.

Damn it, he thought, turning back to the left and grabbing his phone.

Gee, I wonder what time is it? Yeah, 3:22. It figures.

* * *

Thud.

Tibi opened his eyes again. This time, he quickly grabbed his phone.

Silence.

"What time is it?" he mumbled. "Gotta write it down," he added, opening an app.

* * *

"Good morning, babe," said Mia, stretching. "How did you sleep?"

"Good. Good. I mean… I woke up two times. But good."

"Again? What happened? What did you see?"

"Nothing. I mean, I didn't see anything. I just heard some thuds. But it could have been anything."

"Thuds? What kind of thuds? Where were they coming from?"

"I don't know what kind. Deep thuds, I guess. Coming from above. Yes, yes, I know, it could all be in my head. But I wrote down the time it happened both times," he added, getting out of bed and grabbing the camera, "and now we can see together, and *hear* everything."

Tibi pulled out his laptop from his backpack and came back to the bed, stuffing a second pillow underneath his head.

"Come to papa," he murmured as he connected a cable to the camera.

* * *

"What? Impossible!"

"What is it, babe?" asked Mia, giving him a startled glance.

"There's nothing on it," he said, removing his headset. "Look. I mean, listen to this."

Mia closed in and grabbed the headphones.

"Ready?"

She nodded, and Tibi pressed play.

"See how there is some feint background noise. It's me breathing, I guess. And at some point, I will stop when waking up. Then you'll hear me handling the phone on the nightstand and I—"

"Quiet you, I can't hear anything," said Mia, and they both fell silent.

They could see the video on the laptop, and Mia could hear through the headset.

"Yes, I see," she said eventually. "There's nothing there. What did you say it was?"

"A thud! It should have been a loud thud. Coming from above."

"Well, there's nothing there," said Mia, handing Tibi the headset as she got up. "It's sunny outside; let's go out for a walk."

"Just a second. Maybe you want to hear the recording for when the second thud happened. But it's the same. No thud."

* * *

"I still don't understand," said Tibi, as they walked uphill along the main road. "I'm starting to believe it *is* all in my head."

"But everything else doesn't add up then," said Mia.

"You're right. Damn it, you're right."

"What if we bring a priest over?"

"Where? To the room?"

"Yes. But to Room 26, not the one we're in right now. What if the priest can just cast out whatever is lingering there?"

"Like the other priest did in your room," said Tibi, nodding. "That doesn't sound half bad. And if it works, it will be just a strange thing that was somehow connected to that room, then followed me to your home, and a priest cast it out."

"Yup."

"Jesus, the things I'm saying," said Tibi, smiling at Mia. "I can't believe it."

"Why not? There are stronger forces than you and me out there."

"Yeah, I know. I mean, I don't know, but I'm starting to accept there are."

Mia continued to walk in silence, just as the cable car station became visible in the distance.

"I appreciate that you didn't try to convert me just now," said Tibi, looking into his wife's eyes and halting.

"Ha! I think everyone's beliefs are their own. So, if you want to believe in God, like I do, it's fine. And if not, that's fine as well. I do believe you're a good person, so whether you have faith or not, it's of little concern to me."

"I love you so much," said Tibi, and they kissed.

"So, what do we do about that priest?" asked Mia as they resumed their walk uphill.

"I don't know. We need to get ahold of the room. So now it's not a good time. Ah," said Tibi suddenly.

"What?"

"We're getting close to the cable car station."

"So?"

His voice rang hollow as he spoke. "And the gypsy could be there."

"Ah. That's a good idea. We'll ask her what happened three years ago. Do you think she'll remember you?"

"I don't know," said Tibi. "Let's see."

* * *

They approached the tall building and looked around, trying to find the old woman.

"That can't be her," said Mia, pointing at a woman a few dozen feet away. "She's too thin. I don't think she could have lost all that weight. Ah, look," she said as the woman turned around. "It's not her. This one is very young."

"Damn," said Tibi, after a moment's hesitation. "Asking her some questions might have proven useful."

"Why don't you ask this one?"

"This one? But do you think she knows what the other saw?"

"I don't know. What if she can see it as well?" asked Mia, raising her eyebrows while grinning.

"Come on, don't toy with me." Tibi sighed. "Okay, fine. You know what? That's a good idea. I'll go ask her."

Tibi picked up the pace, closely followed by Mia.

As they approached the gypsy, the details of her clothes became clearer. Just like the old woman three years ago, this one had a similar floral dress, only it was gray, with a pattern of red, yellow, white or black flowers printed on it. She was also wearing a matching scarf, and she looked very young.

She had a black, sleeveless, woolen jacket on her back, with an intricate flower-pattern embroidered upon it. The embroidery matched the colors of the flowers on the dress and headscarf.

The gypsy woman was nimble, and every time she moved, the dress swept around, rising and then slowly floating back down to cover her ankles.

As she turned again, this time toward them, they could see the same oval flower basket firmly held under her left arm.

They made eye contact and, instantly, the woman came toward them, talking loudly.

"Ah, hello there, mister! May God have you in His care. Come, buy your pretty miss a bouquet. Look how beautiful she is! She deserves some fragrant flowers, don't you think?"

The woman was clearly young, probably in her early twenties, yet the wind and sun had already started to leave their marks on her still-beautiful face.

"Hello," said Tibi, with a quick smile. "No, I don't want the flowers. I was wondering… I met one of your… colleagues, I guess. An older woman was selling flowers here a few—"

"You did? You should know, mister, that all the flowers we sell are handpicked by us. And we wash and clean, and whatever—"

"No, no, nothing like that," said Tibi, moving his hands in front of him. "No, you've got me all wrong. I have no problem with the flowers or whatever. I just want to talk to the woman."

"Oh, but she's not here anymore, mister. No. Now I am. If you don't mind, I have to sell the flowers and—"

"Look," said Mia, interrupting their exchange and making them both glance her way. "We just want to ask her something. And we're not the police or anything like that."

"Oh, yes, yes," said the woman, taking a few steps back, just as a small child, probably around four years old and wearing poor clothes, reached her and grabbed her dress. "Not to worry, but I have to… I must go home, I think. Yes, that's what I must do." She turned around. "I have to feed my children, yes," she added, pointing to a corner across the street where two other children were sitting on the boardwalk.

An older one, probably about six, was playing with a toddler who didn't look older than two.

"Sorry for bothering you," said Tibi, raising his voice to make sure she heard him. "Have a nice day."

* * *

"Man, that was strange," said Mia later, as they headed back down the road, toward the guesthouse.

"What was? The fact that she seemed afraid?"

"Yes."

"You read too much into it. It's not related to what we're trying to investigate."

"Why do you say that?" said Mia, looking at him.

"She wasn't afraid of me like the other one. The old one saw something that freaked her out. This one was just afraid of us in general. We seemed too inquisitive."

"You think so?"

"Yes. Historically, the police give them a hard time. And even before that, they were oppressed and had to face pure racism, throughout the ages. Plus, I imagine she was selling those flowers without any kind of permit. It's easy to bust her up and take her to the station. She probably feared we were trying to report her."

4 THE GYPSY

"Okay. What do you want to do next?"

"No idea," said Tibi as the Three Bears guesthouse came into view. "We could try the priest thing. Why not?"

"The whole gypsy angle fell apart, I guess," said Mia. "I wonder, if we go back tomorrow, maybe we can find the old lady."

"I don't know. We should go home tomorrow, though. It's Wednesday. Thursday they're expecting me back in the office."

"But we could go quickly in the morning, right?"

"Yes, okay."

"By the way, did you see her children?" asked Mia, turning toward him.

"Yeah. Very poorly dressed."

"Yes, that. But I was talking about their number. And age."

"Ah. Yeah, she looked so young."

"*Very* young. I think she was twenty, maybe even younger. And the oldest one, he was at least five, but probably more like six or seven."

"Yeah, well, it's another culture. What can you do?"

"I know it is, I know. But, man, that's crazy."

"You remember that girl who was in the news, the youngest grandmother in the world?"

"Yeah," said Mia, shaking her head. "That was a gypsy from

51

eastern Europe, too, and I think she was twenty-five."

"Nope. I reckon it was twenty-three."

"Jesus," said Mia, making the sign of the cross.

They continued to advance toward Horza's guesthouse, now only a few dozen yards downhill.

"It's not a bad place," said Tibi, stopping and turning around. "I mean, we have a beautiful view from the window and it's relatively close to the cable car and the trails going up the mountain. Why does it have to be…"

"What? Haunted?"

"I guess. I didn't want to say the word, but, yes." He turned to Mia. "It is haunted, right?"

Mia sighed. "Look, some strange things happened, I agree. But now that I think of it… You basically heard a thud last night. A thud that only you heard, and it wasn't caught on camera."

"Ugh."

"No, babe, don't. Listen to me. What if and, mind me, I'm just asking, *what* if you're just stressing out? I mean, okay, you saw something strange that first night, three years ago. You were tired, we'd had some wine."

"Plus the hot, steamy—"

"Sex, right," said Mia, giggling. "And all this made you very tired. You had a dream, a vivid dream. You hadn't completed your usual exercise routine either, so maybe it was a mix of too much energy and too little sleep? And the intoxication. Maybe it was just a bad dream."

Tibi nodded. "Let's say that's true. What about the following dreams? Were they the same? Just stupid dreams, the result of stress or whatnot?"

"Why not? I mean, now that I think of it," said Mia, grabbing his arm, "it all started with a big, scary dream. All the others were either short or feint sounds, or brief visions."

"So, the first one was a dream, the rest were all in my head?"

"Yes. Exactly. Stress got the best of you. The first disturbing dream led to the following strange dreams."

"And what about the water bottle in your room?"

"Same explanation. Stress. Your subconscious knew about the bottle in the waste basket. And then you slept well because we eliminated the stress, by telling you we got a priest in, to cast away the evil spirits or whatever."

"But don't forget, I'm not a believer. To me, religion is just a construct, created to keep people under control."

"Okay, fine. But you do believe there are some higher forces. Or at least things that we can't always explain, right?"

"Yeah," said Tibi, prolonging the word. "Why?"

"Well, what if, okay, our religion is not the right one. What if it's not really true."

"Or any of the others, for that matter."

"Yes, okay. Let's say none of the existing religions are true. But what if the priests, imams, rabbis, you name it, what if they are somehow holy?"

"Come on," said Tibi with a scowl. "They're all toying with the goodwill and—"

"Yes, yes, but I mean, what if, through all their sermons and rituals and—"

"Mumbo-jumbo."

"Yes, yes, that. What if they do manage to conjure good energies? What if they can pull together the forces of good, and in doing so they manage to push away some bad energies or even entities that might exist?"

Tibi and Mia were walking slowly, holding hands. They were across the street from the guesthouse, just approaching one of the nearby streetlights.

Tibi stopped, grabbed the lamppost with his free hand, and looked at the dark-brown guesthouse.

"Okay. Let's say I... let's say I kind of believe that."

"Well, wouldn't a priest who comes to cast away an evil spirit, or help a restless one find peace, even if he's from a *'wrong'* religion," said Mia, air quoting with her free hand, "give you some inner peace—enough for you to relax and sleep properly?"

"I see what you mean," said Tibi, after a few moments' of thought. "It might be true, okay? I've been thinking about it and considering the scenario that everything is just in my head for a while now. But what about the dreams I've been having? Oh, and what about the gypsy? Not this one, the old one. What was that all about?"

"Coincidence. Who knows what happened back then? What if you looked like someone she knew? What if she thought you were a cop? True, you were rather young to be a cop, or at least an undercover one, but who knows. Maybe it was random. It doesn't have to be related to this."

They spent a few seconds thinking.

Eventually, Tibi turned to look up at the large balcony of their room on the first floor.

"So, we're down there. And above is the room that gave me so much trouble. Why didn't I think three years ago to ask if something had happened in that room?"

"I think you have to let go," said Mia, pulling him closer and making him turn to face her. "It's all in your head. You're in a downward spiral and you need to pull yourself together."

"I think you're right," said Tibi a moment later. He sighed and squeezed her hand. "Come on, let's go eat."

* * *

"You know what," said Tibi, after a B-movie finished on some commercial TV station. "I think you're right. I do feel better. You know? It's like a weight's been lifted. I mean, yeah, I won't lie, I still have a small 'what if'-twinge in my mind. But it's fading." He closed his eyes and drew a deep breath. "And I think it was all in my head."

"That's good," said Mia, kissing him. "So…" she added, pausing while looking at him in a different way, smiling.

"Ah, well, don't mind if I do," he said, reaching for her.

* * *

It was almost midnight and Mia was sleeping.

Tibi put away his phone and closed his eyes. He almost fell asleep, but then he rose, went to his backpack and, with a sigh, took out his cube camera. He positioned it to cover most of the corridor, turned it on, and then went to bed.

* * *

Thud. Thud. Thud.

The thuds repeated a few times, even after his eyes were open.

He looked around the room. There was nothing there. He checked his phone and, again, it was 3:22.

Damn it, he thought. *I really need to get my shit together. I'm too stressed. Same time again?*

Still, he wrote down the time and went back to bed.

As he began to drift off, he kept having a strange feeling, something he couldn't describe. He turned around in the bed to look at Mia, who was sleeping peacefully on her side. Behind her were the large windows leading to the balcony, now fully covered by drapes.

Still, there was a small gap in the curtains through which the light outside was sneaking in. It was just a bit of light, but it somehow stood out in Tibi's mind.

He turned around, setting his back to the window, facing the corridor once more. Then he glanced up, toward the room above. *That damn room. I should never have come here in the first place.*

He suddenly saw the light that was coming in from the balcony window reflecting on the wall that separated the bedroom from the corridor.

That damn light. Reluctantly, he left the warm bed and moved toward the windows. He reached for the drape, to close it. Yet, something made him pull it to the side and look out the window first. His gaze drifted toward the streetlight out front, uphill from the guesthouse.

And, there, he saw her.

A cold shiver moved down his spine and his hand trembled as his grip tightened on the drape.

He leaned closer, squinting as he tried to make out the details.

Yes, it was the gypsy, standing close to the streetlight, a little behind it. And not the young one from today. No, it was definitely the old one, the one from three years ago.

She looked just as he remembered her: very large and dressed in black clothes. There were probably still covered with floral motives, but he was currently too far away to distinguish anything. A headscarf covered her hair and she had a knitted vest coat over her shoulders. She didn't have the basket of flowers with her though.

55

Instead, her hands gripped the coat's openings, where the sleeves should have been.

Then, suddenly, she raised her head and looked straight at him.

Tibi let out a short scream. Meanwhile, the old gypsy was slowly raising her right hand, holding her palm up. She eventually stopped, keeping her hand stretched toward him, and beckoned to him.

Tibi took a quick step back.

Can she see me? She shouldn't be able to. I'm inside, behind the drapes, and it's dark in here.

He turned briefly toward the archway. There was nothing there. Then he quickly looked down at Mia, who was still sleeping.

He thought he heard something from outside, some faint commotion. He looked back out the window, only to see the gypsy walking away slowly, heading uphill. A moment later, he heard a high-pitched voice. Emi must have run out, and now he was shouting, driving the old woman away. "… away … ipsy … police … come back."

Tibi could barely make out what Emi was saying, but the message was clear.

Still, he quickly pulled on some pants, tied his boots and grabbed a jacket. He unlocked the door as quietly as possible. Once out, though, he ran down the stairs to the ground floor.

"Oh, sorry, sir, for the disturbance." Emi's voice was coming from the corridor near the stairs, behind Tibi, his tone apologetic.

"What happened?" asked Tibi over his shoulder, as he continued toward the exit.

"Oh, just some gypsies. It's those damn ones that came to our community a few years ago. They're always on the lookout, scouting for things to steal, I reckon. No, Mr. Coman, you don't have to go after her! I took care of it."

Still, Tibi wasn't paying attention. He exited the building and looked up the street. The row of streetlights extended far into the distance, yet the gypsy was nowhere to be seen.

"Sir," said Emi from the doorway. "What are you doing? It's all right. Look, the car is fine."

"Yes," said Tibi absently, still checking the road uphill. "Yes, I see."

"What's wrong, sir? Come back inside. It's cold. And don't

worry: we are in a safe place."

A few moments passed; Tibi was still looking into the distance.

"I'll go inside; it's cold. I'll leave the door unlocked. Please lock it behind you when you return," said Emi. "Goodnight, sir."

"Oh, goodnight," said Tibi a moment later, when Emi's words finally filtered through. It was only then he realized he was alone in front of the guesthouse, and he could finally feel the cold.

Knock, knock.

He turned around, looking up the building. Was there a knock coming from one of the windows? He glanced at his room, and then the one above. He could see nothing at any of the windows.

Did my mind just make up a knock? God damn it, he thought, returning to the front door of the guesthouse as his muscles started to tremble, trying to fight the cold. *I'm getting really stressed.*

* * *

"Good morning, babe," said Mia, kissing Tibi gently.

"Oh, good morning, sweetie," said Tibi, yawning. "Did you sleep well?"

"Yes, I sure did. How about you?"

"You'll never guess who I saw last night."

"Who? Don't tell me, the black… shadow?"

"No, no," said Tibi, forcing a laugh. "No, it was the gypsy."

"What? What do you mean? Did you dream about the gypsy? The young one, I hope," said Mia, giggling.

"No, no. I saw, out the window, the old one. The one from three years ago. And, yes, before you ask, I think I saw the dark mole below her left eye. I mean, she was far away, but for a moment she looked straight at me."

"What? Jesus. Are you sure that wasn't… you know, a dream?"

"Yes, yes. Emi was there as well. We talked. You can ask him."

"Wow, Jesus. This is really strange. Okay, and what did the gypsy want?"

"She just made a sign, beckoning me to follow her. Or to go to her. I don't know."

"Damn. That's scary. What did you do?"

"I went after her, of course."

"Really? Jesus, you're crazy," said Mia, accompanying her words with a short laugh. "What if they were there to rob you?"

"No, no. I don't think so. Besides, Emi scared her off before I could find her."

"Damn," said Mia, shaking her head. "This is a strange place. I'm so glad we're going home. I don't want to come back here ever again."

"I hear you," said Tibi, nodding. "Let's go eat. And… I was thinking—"

"Yes, yes, we'll do as we discussed. We'll go to the cable car and try to meet the gypsy."

"Good. But first, I want to check the camera. I woke at 3:22. I heard those thuds again. Yes, yes, I know, it's probably just my imagination. But I still want to see if the recording captured anything."

As expected, there was nothing on the camera that could point to a real thud happening.

* * *

After a hefty meal composed of plenty of eggs and white cheese, they reached the cable car station. They looked around but couldn't find any gypsy, whether young or old.

"Damn it," said Mia. "I really hoped we could find the old one. If she called you out last night, why isn't she here?"

"I'll ask," said Tibi, going to the ticket office. "Excuse me," he said, leaning into the opening. "About the gypsy women who hang around here, selling flowers—"

"Ah, to hell with them," said the woman. "They're always here, scaring the customers. Did you notice how bad they smell? It's like a campfire. They're up to no good. And if you want flowers, you're better off not giving them ten Euros for those flimsy bouquets. Just go anywhere around our town and there are plenty of flowers for everyone. And mind your pockets. Yeah, they steal not just by selling cheap-ass flowers for a fortune. They are thieves."

"Okay, thank you," said Tibi, backing off. "Sheesh," he then said to Mia. "Man, that one really hates them."

"Yeah, well. We don't know what's going on in this town, or

what history they have together."

"Let's go back home. To hell with this place," said Tibi, and they set off toward the guesthouse.

* * *

"Hey, Emi," said Tibi, throwing a quick smile at the young man behind the counter. "Sorry about yesterday."

"What—"

"We have to go, but I wanted to ask you about Room 26."

"What about it?" asked Emi, looking puzzled.

"I'd like to book it."

"Why? I mean, okay. Was there something wrong with Room 16?"

"No, no," said Tibi, waving his hands. "We loved the room. But I would like to spend more time in Room 26. Let's just say it's for sentimental reasons."

"Okay," said Emi, glancing at the papers in front of him. For a moment it looked like he wanted to write something but wasn't sure what. "So… for what period do you wish to book the room?"

"The first available weekend," said Tibi.

"I guess we're coming back?" whispered Mia, drawing Tibi to the side, while Emi checked the large notebook.

"I was thinking that, to do this properly and put it to bed once and for all, we should come for two days and sleep in Room 26. I'll convince myself it was just a dream, then we'll go home and I'll move on. And, yes, I want to use the camera as well."

"Jesus. Okay. But I thought we'd already agreed it was just in your head?"

"That gypsy coming here last night… that was a bit… It was disturbing. Sorry I didn't talk to you in advance, but I need this. If you really don't want to come back here, I can come alone."

"No, no, I'm not saying that," said Mia, just as Horza approached, coming from a room out back.

"Oh, hello. Checking out? I hope you enjoyed your stay," he said with a quick, almost fake smile.

"Yes," said Emi instantly, looking at him. "They loved it so much, they want to come back again. To stay in Room 26."

"Oh," said Horza with a vacant expression. "Why Room 26?" he asked, turning to Tibi.

"No real reason," he said, glancing at Mia.

She moved her eyes in a specific way that made Tibi understand something.

"Look," he said, turning back to Horza and Emi. "I had some strange dreams in that room three years ago. I know it sounds odd, but that thing has been haunting me ever since."

"Oh," said Horza, in a raspy voice. "I see. What kind of dreams?"

"Some shadow, a tall man. Look, I know how that sounds," added Tibi, as Emi and Horza exchanged quick glances. "And, believe me, I want to get it out of my head. But the gypsy last night was the last straw. I really need some closure."

"What gypsy last night?" asked Horza.

"The one Emi chased away," said Tibi.

"What?" Emi squeaked, sounding even more high-pitched than usual. "No. I didn't chase away any gypsies. I don't know what he's talking about."

"Look," said Horza, raising his hand as everyone was about to start talking at once. "We thank you for your business. We'll call you when we have an opening for Room 26. Okay?"

Everybody nodded.

"We have their numbers, yes, Emi?"

"Yes."

"Fine. Have a safe trip," said Horza, with a smile as fake as the Rosenthal vase on the front desk.

* * *

"What the hell," said Tibi, huffing as he drove slowly downhill. "He made me look like an idiot."

"Who?"

"Emi. And he basically called me a liar."

"What do you mean?"

"How he said he didn't chase away that gypsy. Pfft. I looked like a rambling lunatic, didn't I?"

"Well…" said Mia, smiling. "I mean, sorry," she added, giggling, "but you asked."

"He talked to me for a while when I went out to find her. I could barely shake him off."

"Don't tell me he was still at his desk!"

"No, no. I think he came from his room out back."

"Ah, so he does sleep. I guess you finally saw him wearing something other than those grandpa clothes?"

"No. Hmm, now that I think about it, I never looked at him. He was always behind me, and I was always looking for the old gypsy. Still, he was there and he lied about it."

"His behavior was strange. Maybe Horza is strict about that subject. But good thing we're out of there. And I don't know why you want to come back again. We should have talked about it first."

"Yes. Sorry. I just had the impulse. It just got to me."

"Anyway, I don't think they'll call."

"You don't?" asked Tibi.

"No. I think you made quite an impression—one strong enough to keep us away from them forever," said Mia, snickering.

5 BLOOD

He was in the woods, looking for something. His shovel struck the ground again and again. Suddenly, he hit something hard.

He woke up, gasping.

"What is it, babe?" said Mia, turning toward him.

"Nothing."

"That dream again?"

"Yeah. But don't worry. Go to sleep."

Tibi left the bedroom to get a glass of water. He checked the time and sighed.

"Damn it," he mumbled, sitting on the couch in the living room.

* * *

"That's not good, man," said Mike, taking a bite from his croissant. "I'm starting to think you need to see a shrink. And after you start eating like normal people, maybe he can help you fix that sleeping problem as well."

"Oh, stop it already," said Tibi, looking glum.

"Hey, sorry, man. I was just pulling your leg, you know?"

"Yeah, yeah. I'm not in the mood. This shit is serious."

"It is, it is. It's been six months already since you saw that old gypsy woman by the lamppost. You should listen to Mia and let it go. The old woman is just messing with your head."

"But there are so many—"

"Look, even those guys from the guesthouse never called back, right? I guess they also think you need to chill out."

"Who, Emi and Horza?" asked Tibi, turning to Mike. "No, man, they didn't call. They said they would, but I guess Mia was right."

"Why don't *you* call *them*? I mean, you need some closure. Just call them, ask them over the phone if there's something strange about that room. Then you'll see there's nothing to worry about. And I'm telling you, you look like shit, you know?"

"Gee, thanks! But you're right! I'm tired. I'm afraid to go to bed, and I haven't been to the gym at all the last few weeks."

"That's not good, man," said Mike, reaching for his third croissant. "Exercise is important. I think," he added, laughing.

"You're lucky you're young, you know?"

"What, is that a fat joke? I've read that it's better to feel good about your body and be a bit overweight than to be thin and stress about being fit. You'll live longer if you're happy."

"I'm starting to believe that's true," said Tibi, sighing as he reached for his phone.

"You gonna call them?"

"Yeah. There's nothing else I can— Oh, hello? Yes, hi Emi. It's me, Tibi. Yes, Mr. Coman, but, as I've said before, you can call me Tibi. Yes, I'm calling about... ah, yes, you remembered... Yes, I know it's Easter this weekend, but don't you have anything else... I see. Afterwards? Nothing until September? Really? Well, can you talk to Mr. Horza, please? Better yet, do you have his phone number? Oh... Okay. But how about another room? Do you have one? Any weekend, really. I'd prefer Room 26, but I guess it's fully booked. Yes, please check. Why can't you check now? Okay, okay. I'll wait for your call."

"They'll never call," said Mike, finishing off the fourth croissant. "Are you sure you don't want the last one?"

* * *

The phone rang around midday. Tibi grabbed it eagerly.

"Hello? Yes, hi Emi. Yes. What? What do you mean? But when's the first available… Oh, come on, Emi. I'm telling you, I want to put this to bed… This is not fair, man, not fair at all!"

He threw the phone onto the desk.

"What?" asked Mike, turning from his LCDs.

Tibi's voice caught in his throat. "They've banned me from ever going back to the guesthouse."

Mike started laughing, loudly, holding his large belly.

"To hell with you too," said Tibi, trying to control himself but letting out a stifled laugh. "Why are you laughing?"

"Oh, man," said Mike, wiping a few tears, "they must think you're a nutjob. I mean, I already knew that, ever since the whole 'chickens are people too' thing you have going on, but, man, this is next level."

Tibi was silent for a few minutes, fidgeting with his mouse, not actually doing anything.

"I'll take a room at another guesthouse in the same resort," he said eventually, making Mike turn toward him once more.

"What? Why?"

"I'm going to track down that old gypsy."

* * *

"Oh, come on, Tibi," said Mia, taking a sip from her wine glass. "Why would you do that?"

"I have to, Mia. I do. I can't explain. I'm going crazy."

Mia was silent for a moment, toying with her glass. "You're changing, that's true," she said at last, setting down her drink. "We haven't made love in a month now. What's wrong?"

"*This* is wrong! Sorry. I didn't mean to yell. I'm very tired and I don't sleep well. I really have to solve this thing."

"But they're just dreams! Can't you accept that's what they are?"

"I've tried. Don't you think I've tried? But they seem so real. So real! And it is the same, identical dream, over and over again. And it's been three years now, almost four actually, and I think I'm going crazy. I have to find that gypsy, ask her what the hell is happening to me, and then leave all this shit behind."

Mia pondered as she checked her husband's face and posture. "You're right. And we're in this together. We need to solve this. It's damaging our lives. When do you want to go?"

"As soon as possible. It's Wednesday, so maybe we can go this weekend."

"But it's Easter. You know how it gets. They'll all get into their cars and move entire cities to small towns in the mountains. I don't know if it's an East-European thing or not, but it's always crazy packed."

"Yes, but maybe I can still find something. There are other guesthouses out there, you know."

"Okay, fine. Try to find something. I can join you for Easter, even if we've previously discussed not getting into the huge traffic jams together with the herd."

Tibi spent a few dozen minutes looking up accommodation over the internet and then placing calls.

"Damn it!" he said, as he got off the phone. "Nothing for a few weeks."

"How many have you called?"

"I don't know. Too many to remember. Probably a dozen. I have a few more, but if none of them have availability…"

Tibi placed another call, then returned to Mia, happy.

"Perfect!" he exclaimed. "I've found one that has an opening starting Monday, second day of Easter. Pointy Nose Bed & Breakfast or something like that. Strange name. Someone just cancelled, so we can take that room."

"Damn, but I can't leave after Easter. You know how it is. People eat piles of food and then decide they'll do something about it. So the first couple of weeks after Easter all the gyms are full. I can't go then."

"Damn. We can wait for three weeks, I guess." Tibi didn't sound too convinced.

"I can probably go next week, but I'm not sure now. It depends on what happens this weekend. Who knows, maybe it will be different this year."

"I don't think so," said Tibi, shaking his head. "People here never learn."

"I have the same feeling," said Mia, smiling weakly.

"Ugh. I could go alone, if that's okay with you. I'll go in on Monday evening, so we can spend most of the day together. I'll find the gypsy early the next day, talk to her and then come straight home."

"Fine," said Mia, after a while. "If it helps, let's do it. But please, please be careful!"

* * *

Tibi pulled up in front of another inn, a few hundred yards closer to the cable car station than Horza's.

He got out, taking in the mountain's cold, fresh air. He grabbed his duffle bag and, without looking around, entered the guesthouse, immediately making eye contact with the woman in the lobby.

She was in her thirties, dressed in a warm, colored sweater and jeans.

"Oh, Mr. Coman, hello sir. Welcome to our guesthouse," she said with a wide smile.

"Hello Ms. Capata," said Tibi, trying a quick smile himself. "Please call me Tibi. And I'm sorry to have arrived so late. I hope the room is still available."

"Ah, yes, of course. And don't you worry; it's fine with us. You arrive when you want and you leave whenever you want. Of course, as long as it happens this Sunday, before noon," added the lady, with a laugh.

"Ha! Yes," said Tibi, smiling genuinely for the first time. "Don't worry about that. I won't overstay my welcome. I might just leave sooner, you know."

"Oh," said the woman, becoming a bit puzzled.

"I'll pay for the entire period, of course," said Tibi.

"We'll see," said the woman. "If we can find another guest, we'll find a way to be fair to everybody. Just let us know. Do you want to eat with us in the morning?" she added, a smile returning to her tanned face. "We're not a restaurant, only a small family-owned inn, but we can prepare local food for you, which you can eat in the dining room or even out in the gazebo."

"Local food sounds great," said Tibi. "The only thing is, I'm a vegetarian. So it might not be—"

"Oh, don't you worry, Mr. Coman."

"Tibi."

"Yes, Tibi. We have plenty of food without meat. How about eggs and cheese?"

"Yes, that sounds good."

"Perfect! Oh, by the way, my name is Ana. Call me if you need anything."

"Hi Ana," said Tibi, extending his hand and shaking the owner's.

"Now, let me show you to your room."

They reached the first floor, where Anna showed him a quaint but cozy room. The inn's first and only floor was all wood, and the interior was decorated in the same way as the rest of the house. It had warm, soothing oak colors, with knitted rugs and carpets everywhere. Even the walls were covered with hung tapestries depicting scenes from *The Abduction from the Seraglio*, this time in vivid colors.

"This is perfect," said Tibi, dropping his duffle bag.

"Do you want some food this evening?" asked Ana. "It's almost ten, but I think we can find some vegetarian goodies in our pantry. I can even whisk up some polenta with a bit of fresh cheese and sour cream."

"That sounds perfect, thank you," said Tibi. "That would really help, as I'm beat."

"No problem," said Ana, turning fast and hurrying down the stairs. "I'll call you in about fifteen minutes."

∗ ∗ ∗

"This is one of the best dinners I've ever had," said Tibi, setting down the fork and leaning back in his chair. "I'm full."

"I'm happy to hear that," said Ana, grabbing the plates. "Just let me know if you need anything else."

"No, it was more than… Actually, maybe you could help me with something else."

"Yes?" asked Ana, stopping on her way back to the kitchen.

"Oh, don't let me hold you up. Sorry. You can take those to the kitchen and if you still have five minutes after, we can talk."

∗ ∗ ∗

"So, Mr. Coman, what do you want to know?" asked Ana, sitting down at the table, having returned a few moments ago with a small plate of honeycomb pieces and two teaspoons.

"First, I'm curious about the name of your guesthouse."

"Oh, that," said Ana, giggling.

"The Pointy Nose Bed & Breakfast sounds rather strange. And, looking at the interior, it's a really traditional and rustic place."

"Indeed. It was initially a bit different. We bought it off the previous owners, me and my husband," said Ana, grabbing a small piece of honeycomb. "The previous owners had more of a Halloween theme going, you know, with Strigoi, Moroi and Iele all over the place. You know, some sort of vampires, zombies and witches showcased everywhere."

"Yeah, I know about the local folklore," said Tibi.

"Right. But we are good Christians and we didn't like any of that. So we changed the interior design to how it is now."

"I see. But you liked the name?"

"Indeed. It was somehow funny, and I think people remember it easily. You know, all guesthouses here have some kind of animal name, like The Two Stags or The Woodchucks, or maybe just the owner's name. Imagine, this could have been 'Ana's Inn' or 'The Three Squirrels' or something."

"You're right. The name does make it rather unique," said Tibi, grabbing some honeycomb.

"Indeed it does. That's all you wanted to know?"

"No. I also wanted to ask you about the gypsies who come around this village from time to time."

"Oh… that's an unexpected interest," said Ana, laughing. "Sure, ask away."

"I want to know where I could find them."

"Ah, you can find them everywhere, I think, but mostly around the market, at the cable car and—"

"No, no. I mean, where are they living? Where do they spend the night? Do they rent something around here?"

"Ah, that. May I ask you first why are you so interested in them?"

"I have… I need to… Look, I feel like I can trust you, I don't know why. I want to solve a mystery."

"Mystery?"

"Yes. It's a bit strange. Something happened to me and I think it involves the gypsies around here."

"Are you with the government?"

"What? No, no. It's not that kind of 'mystery'," said Tibi, doing air quotes and then reaching again for his teaspoon. "This is good honeycomb, thank you," he added a few moments later.

"You're welcome. Okay. I guess what happened is, let's say, private," said Ana, and Tibi nodded. "Okay. So, you asked where they live. The ones around here are the nomadic kind. They set up an encampment about four or five years ago, up the mountain. Four years, I think. It's quite a long time, I guess, for people who are called 'nomadic'," said Ana, laughing again. "I don't know exactly where, but I know someone who does. If you want, I can ask tomorrow morning, when I pick up my supplies."

"Yes, please do. What else do you know about them?"

"You know, this and that. There were some petty thefts that people think were related, but none were proven. Most of the time they make money working as day laborers here and there, selling mushrooms in the market, or flowers by the cable car station. And I think they tried to sell some chickens once, live ones, but very few people were eager to buy from them. And, don't worry, the food I give you— Oh, I forgot, you're not into meat. But anyway, everything you get here will have come from our local farmers."

"Great," said Tibi.

"Oh, and some of the women are fortunetellers. They do Tarot and palm reading. The priest always said they were dealing with the occult, though, so we don't want to have anything to do with them. Pagan beliefs, really, even black magic—things that endanger your soul."

"I see. Okay. Could you please find out where their camp is? I'd like to pay them a visit."

"Are you sure, Mr. Coman?"

"Tibi, please. I'm too young to be called 'Mr'."

"Right, okay. Tibi, I don't think they would cause any problems, but going to their camp all alone…" said Ana, shaking her head and squeezing her lips. "That spells trouble to me."

"You said they didn't make any trouble when working around the town."

"Yes, as day laborers and roustabouts. They get very little pay for small jobs around the house and garden. I'll ask my husband when he's back from his trip, but I would advise caution."

"Yes, of course. I won't go there and be disrespectful or aggressive. I just need to talk to someone who is in that camp, that's all. Unless I can find her at the cable car."

"Oh," said Ana, blushing a bit. "I hope you're not in some kind of trouble."

"No, no, nothing like that," said Tibi, waving his hand. "It's an old woman I'm looking for. She used to sell flowers, but last time I checked she wasn't there anymore."

"Okay," said Ana, rising up from the table and grabbing the now-empty plate. "I'll wish you goodnight, and tomorrow I'll ask around about the location of the campsite."

* * *

"Hey babe," came Mia's voice over the phone. "How are you?"

"I'm fine. I arrived safely and I've had an amazing dinner prepared by Ana, the owner."

"Ana, hmm," said Mia. "How's Ana? Is she cute?"

"She is cute, yes," said Tibi, grinning. "Brownish hair, green eyes. But she has a big nose. Too large for my taste."

"Really?" said Mia, bursting into laughter. "And her inn is called Pointy Nose?"

"Ha, ha! I didn't realize that. Do you think there's a connection?"

"You tell me," said Mia, continuing to laugh. "You could ask her."

"I actually did ask her. She said it's an old name and they just kept it. Anyway, she seems like a good person, but don't worry, you're the only one I think about."

"That's good. So, you'll turn in for the night?"

"Yes, of course. I'm beat. But you know, this place, it's better than the other one. Okay, it's more rustic, but this guesthouse is in better taste. The interior has a welcoming design and it feels more like belonging to the place, you know? We should come here at some point."

70

"Yeah, I know what you mean. And, yes, we'll go there. Why not."

"I really like it here. Goodnight, my love," said Tibi, making a few kissing sounds.

"Goodnight, babe. Sleep tight. Call me tomorrow."

* * *

"Good morning, Tibi," said Ana, coming into the dining room. "Would you like to try our eggs?" she asked, putting down a bowl containing three hardboiled eggs, their shells painted red for Easter.

"Yes, thank you."

"Coffee or tea?"

"Black tea, please."

"Right away," said Ana, turning around.

As Tibi ate, he sent a few messages to Mia, who was on her way to her gym.

"I found out what you asked me to," said Ana, setting down a cup filled with hot water and a tea bag.

"Yes? Please, tell me."

"Apparently, they move a lot, but they seem to stay around this area. They never stray too far, and for the last five years they've always kept within a relatively short walking distance from our village. Still, the information is not that fresh, so they might have moved away for good during the last few weeks."

"Damn. I hope they're still around here."

"For your sake, me too. So, it's rather simple. You go up the main road, until you reach the cable car station. From there, follow the path under the cables of the cable car until you reach the stream. It's small, but you can't miss it. Then follow the brook up the mountain and, at some point, there should be a clearing to the left."

"So, that should be on the right side of the river?"

"Yeah, if you take the standard way of naming the left and right sides of a river," said Ana, smiling widely. "But to you, it's going to be on your left. Since, you know, you'll be going up."

"Yes, that sounds clear enough," said Tibi, removing the teabag from his cup and taking a sip. "This is good tea, thank you."

"You're welcome. So, there, at the clearing, you should find the campsite. You won't miss it if you follow these instructions."

"Great," said Tibi. "Thanks a lot for your help."

"No problem. Are you sure you want to do this though?" asked Ana, suddenly sounding wary. "Do you want to take a policeman with you? My brother-in-law, Julian, is in the force. I could ask him to send—"

"No, no, thank you. You're very kind, but I don't want to go there with the cavalry. I'm just a simple man, asking a few questions."

"Okay, suit yourself then," said Ana, rising up from the table. "Oh, I forgot to mention. It's within walking distance, but it's rather a long hike uphill—about three miles. So it will take a couple of hours to get there."

* * *

Tibi reached the cable car station. He was looking around at the people standing in line, waiting to board the next car, when suddenly his phone rang.

"Oh, hey, honey," said Tibi, answering it. "How's the gym?"

"It's crowded," came the answer. "I'm sorry I can't be with you. What are you doing now, babe?"

"I'm trying to find a gypsy at the cable car station, but I can't see any. I so hope they didn't move their camp."

"Hmm, so they *are* nomadic ones?"

"Yeah. I mean, I talked to Ana. She told me a lot of things about them. I'm on my way to look for their camp now. I'll call you after I finish."

* * *

He reached the stream. Ana was right: it was as small as a creek. It was about 10am, and the sun was shining brightly through the trees.

Still, Tibi didn't spend too much time admiring the beautiful surroundings, and he almost stepped on a few snowdrops as he climbed the mountain.

"Oops," he said, barely missing them. "Sorry, little ones," he added. Then he squeezed his backpack straps tighter and headed on.

As he walked uphill, he suddenly saw something and stopped.

"So, I'm going in the right direction," he mumbled, looking at a well-worn trail on his side of the creek. There were footprints everywhere, some of them visible even in the few small patches of snow. *They must be walking this path daily, to sell those damn flowers and chickens.*

He continued his advance and two hours quickly passed by.

Suddenly, across the creek to the left, he saw an opening between the trees. It looked like a tunnel, leading to a larger space on the other side of the thicket.

"Nice," he said, jumping the creek and confidently stepping between the trees.

A few dogs started barking loudly as he approached the open space.

He had reached the campsite, but Tibi had no time to check it out. Two dogs came running, and Tibi halted abruptly when he saw them.

Shit. I don't even have a stick, he thought, quickly looking around for something he could grab.

The two dogs got to a dozen feet away, then kept their distance, still barking loudly. As if the move was coordinated, three more dogs came running from the camp out back and, soon enough, Tibi was surrounded by five large hounds. They were all wooly and gray, and saliva and spit were coming out of their snapping snouts with each loud bark.

"Easy," said Tibi, slowly turning around while holding his arms away. "Eaaasy."

"Beshes!" came a loud yell, as a few men came running from the camp. "Jucal, ja!"

The dogs returned to the camp as the men swung large clubs, almost hitting a few of them.

"Ja, ja!" yelled one of the men, and then, with the dogs subdued, the three men turned toward Tibi, just as four more arrived from the campsite.

"What want?" asked one of the gypsies.

Tibi took a deep breath while sizing up the seven men gathered around him. They were all brown, muscular yet skinny, with large moustaches covering their upper lips. They had three-day beards and their dark hair was combed back. Some of them were wearing wide-brimmed black hats, leather vests and worn-out cloth pants. Their black leather boots were confidently stuck in the muddy ground. Most of them had large clubs, though some had shovels and one was even holding a sword. All of them had knives at their belts. They all had visible scars and bruises across their arms and faces, while the one who had spoken also had a long red scar that went from below his left eye down to his upper lip.

As the young men approached, Tibi registered the smell of smoke coming from them.

Involuntarily, he went into a passive fighting stance. He moved his hands forward, in front of his face, yet tried to be as unaggressive as possible, keeping his palms facing outward. He took a quick step back with his right foot.

"Hello, everyone," said Tibi, looking at each of the seven men in turn as they surrounded him. He bowed his head briefly. "I come in peace. Not looking for trouble."

"What want?" asked the same gypsy once more. He seemed to be the oldest, but their sun- and rain-beaten faces made it difficult to guess their ages.

"I want to speak… There was a woman, who came down to the cable car station from here."

A groan came from a few of the men, who took a step closer to Tibi.

"Wait! Wait! It's not like that. I only want to talk to her. She's an old lady, a grandmother."

"You go away!" said the gypsy. "Go! Ja! Ja!" he added, pushing his club toward Tibi.

"Hey, man, come on. I'm not here to harm anyone. Look, can I talk to the Bulibasa? That's the term, right, for the leader of a gypsy clan or group? He's the law around here, right? Can I talk to him?"

The seven gypsies looked at each other, until the oldest one spoke again. In his dialect, he said something to the other men, then he turned back toward the campsite and started walking.

Everyone else stood still, waiting, and Tibi finally had some time to take a look at the clearing in front of him.

A few wagons and gray tents covered a fifty-yard diameter circle.

They were placed in such a way that he couldn't see inside the circle. Still, a few smoke trails were rising straight up: a sign that there were quite a lot of people in the middle.

The men surrounding him kept a watchful eye on him, and each of them looked more than capable of putting up a good fight.

Suddenly, the oldest one returned, said a few things in his dialect, then turned to Tibi.

"Bulibasa see you. Come."

Tibi followed the man into the camp. As he walked the few dozen steps, he saw a few more details from the campsite. The gray carts were partially covered, and inside he noticed improvised beds. The tents were closed off.

Tibi stepped inside the circle. There, he saw three large campfires. Coincidence or not, he could swear they formed an equilateral triangle. A few dozen chickens were moving around freely, while the neighs of several horses could be heard coming from behind the farthermost carts and tents.

The smell was poignant, and it was a combination of smoke, wet chicken, horse manure and strange spices.

Around the campfire in the back sat eight older men, and Tibi was being led toward them.

To the left was another large campfire, surrounded by about a dozen men, with plenty of empty spots around it. To the right was the third campfire, where a few women of mixed ages were cooking something in a large cauldron.

Everyone looked at Tibi, who raised his hand, waving shyly at them. He quickly put his hand down, though, as the older man showing him the way stopped, bowed his head quickly, then started talking to the group of eight.

During the exchange, the six others guarding him took a few steps back.

"Speak," said the older man eventually, then moved away to join the others.

Tibi looked at the eight men around the fire, but one of them caught his attention. He was bulky and he seemed gigantic, sitting down on a few rugs. He had a large mustache and several thick, gold chains around his neck. His clothes were made of leather and knitted wool, and he had a sheepskin vest on his back. At his belt, a large curved knife was tucked into a gold-plated sheath.

The other men seemed rather skinny, all of them lazily smoking something that had a powerful smell. All wore golden chains around their necks and large, thick rings on their brown fingers.

"Hello, Mr. Bulibasa," said Tibi, with a quick nod to the man who seemed to be in charge.

The large man remained silent and continued to glare at Tibi.

"I came here to ask for your help." Tibi paused for a moment, yet no one flinched. He then continued, a bit less confidently, "I have met a woman from your campsite. An old woman, mind you," he quickly added as a few of the people around the fire turned their glances toward the Bulibasa. "She said something to me before, and I want to talk further with her."

Still, no one said anything. He could hear the fire crackling and even the women around the other fire were silent.

"Would you please help me? I need her help. Could you invite her here, so we can talk?"

"No women at council." Bulibasa's voice was deep and his words prompted a nod from the other seven men.

"Oh, right. Can I go to the other campfire then and—"

"No men at women fire."

"Yes, yes. But can we meet somewhere in between? I only have a few questions."

The men around the fire talked for a few minutes. A few seemed to get a bit angry, others were more restrained. Still, Bulibasa said nothing during this time.

"Look," said Tibi, louder. The chatter stopped and everyone turned to him. "I have these dreams and one of your women, a member of your community, saw something in me. She's an old lady and she had a dark mole, a mark underneath her left eye," said Tibi, touching his left cheek as he felt his confidence returning. "I just want to talk to her, so she can tell me what she saw. I will pay for the trouble, of course," he added, touching his left pocket.

The men looked at each other again, then resumed their chatter.

"Woman not with us," said Bulibasa suddenly, and everyone grew quiet. "But you have bad omen. Baba look at you."

Immediately, the man with the large scar came closer and signaled for Tibi to follow him. Tibi nodded to the group of eight and followed the man, just as a very old gypsy woman approached them, coming from one of the tents. The man said a few words then went away, and Tibi was left alone with Baba.

"Hello," said Tibi, looking at the old woman. It wasn't the one with the mole, but maybe this one could help too. She looked very old, and golden coins were woven into her braided, white-gray hair. A scarf covered the top of her head, and her clothes were made from the same fabric: black with floral motives.

"Oh, hello young man," she said, assessing him from head to toe. She spoke better than all the others so far, yet she still retained a strong accent. "You tell Baba what's troubling—" She suddenly looked at his face, abruptly stopping mid-sentence. "I see," she said, spitting a few times to her left. "You have the omen. And the evil eye. You have seen it. And you share the blood."

"What? What have I seen? What do I share? And what's that about the evil eye?"

"Someone has done this to you."

"Well… Can you undo it?"

"I can undo the evil eye. But the omen, only you can."

"What can I do?"

"You have to make a pact. If you make it, you will fix it. And then you'll be free. Only this way you can do it."

Tibi said nothing, looking into the old woman's deep, black eyes. "This is all very strange. You speak in riddles. I'm not sure I understand."

"What do you want?"

"I want the dreams to stop," said Tibi. "I'm not sure about a pact. A pact with whom? I just hope you're not talking about a pact with the devil."

"No, no," said the old woman, shaking her head, yet her eyes continued to drill through Tibi's. "No. It's a pact for the omen. It will help it go away. God will help you."

"Yes. Fine. I want that."

"Good, good," said the old lady, looking behind him. She said a few words in her dialect, and then turned around, leaving.

"What the… But can you tell me a bit more about—"

"Come," said the man with the cut across his face. "Come, follow."

Tibi had to return to the Bulibasa's fire. He looked toward Baba, called her a few times, but she left without glancing back.

Tibi's guardian pulled him to the council. He talked to the eight and then left, but not before bowing his head briefly.

"Good," said the Bulibasa, "you will make the pact."

"Yes, but I'd like to—"

"Great," said Bulibasa, turning for the first time to his side. He said a few words to his left, a bit louder than usual.

Instantly, a few women got up from their circle. They moved to the side, where a few baskets stood. Some seemed to be dug into the ground. They opened them up and took out chicken eggs, putting them into a large metal bowl. The bowl seemed to be handmade, as it had facets that looked struck by a hammer.

A few young girls, no older than ten, ran away behind the carts and tents. They were all barefoot and their little feet left small footprints in the cold, spring mud.

"Sit," said the Bulibasa, getting Tibi's attention.

"What?"

"I said sit." The Bulibasa was pointing at a small rug laid beside the fire by the man with the scarred cheek.

"Oh, but maybe the women need some help with—"

"That woman job," said Bulibasa, laughing as the others joined him. "Sit. Smoke," he added, as another one at the council handed him a pipe.

Tibi sat down, inspecting the pipe that had been in some old guy's mouth just seconds ago. *Damn it. I must show friendliness. I mustn't show I'm disgusted,* he thought, trying to control his face.

He took a short drag, held it in, then coughed a few times. The eight men around the fire smiled.

Tibi continued to smoke, taking a look back toward the circle, just as the women started boiling the eggs.

Dozens of minutes passed, and Tibi was feeling dizzy. *There must be something in this tobacco we're smoking,* he thought, looking around at the council.

He wasn't a smoker. Yet he knew enough to realize this was a mild one. Anyone could smoke it and, save for the initial cough, he'd quickly got used to it. The smelly pipe had plenty of holes in it, so the smoke was pretty diluted by the time it entered his lungs.

Suddenly, Bulibasa said a few words, again a bit louder, and the man with the scar on his face came a moment later with a wooden casket and nine wooden mugs, all caried in a large wooden half-barrel.

He poured a reddish liquid and shared the mugs, giving Tibi the second one, right after Bulibasa got his.

The eight men of the council drank it and the man with the scar started to refill their cups.

Who is this guy, their servant? thought Tibi, looking at the man.

"Do you have a name?" asked Tibi, yet the man didn't answer. A few of the eight looked at him.

Damn. I hope I didn't put him in the spotlight.

"Cheers," said Tibi, trying a smile, yet no one joined him. He took a sip and a strange smell and taste invaded his senses. This wasn't wine, nor anything he'd ever tasted before. Yet it was clearly alcoholic, long and with a strong flavor. It reminded him of a plant bitter: the kind of non-alcoholic herbal drink his mom used to give him before lunch occasionally when he was a child.

He followed what the others were doing and drank the entire mug, quickly receiving a refill.

Suddenly, three other women got up, just as Tibi was looking to his right for the hundredth time. They walked around the improvised yard, grabbed one chicken each and, with quick, skillful moves, cut their heads off.

At the same time, the woman handling the eggs retrieved the metal bowl from the wood fire using large tongs and poured the hot water into a smaller bowl.

The three women closed in and squeezed the blood from the chickens on top of the boiled eggs, holding the chickens still as they struggled in their arms before finally become stiff.

Tibi flinched with disgust at the thought of those eggs drenched in raw chicken blood.

Then the three women approached the smaller bowl, the one with the hot water. They squatted and each started plucking the feathers from their chickens.

* * *

Tibi was dizzy. Was it the drink—he'd downed three mugs already—or the smoking, which he'd done constantly for the last hour? Perhaps it was a combination of both.

He felt good though. His stress had melted away, and he soon found himself smiling as he looked around.

The ten-year-old girls came back then, skipping between the carts and tents. They were all carrying something muddy in their hands.

They gathered in the middle of the yard, putting together something on the ground. Tibi tried to see what it was, but it was impossible to make out. He was seated, the girls were behind him, and he got dizzy when he tried to turn his head.

After a few moments, they seemed to finish their work, and they moved on to other tasks. One grabbed a shovel and started digging a hole in the ground, next to the place where they'd placed the mud from their hands. The shovel was large, too large for her, but she continued her work, pushing the spade with her bare feet.

The others grabbed the bowl with blood-red eggs and started peeling them. All the egg shells went into another bowl, and soon enough they had a few dozen eggs, all peeled, and a large bowl with red shell in it.

The girls then grabbed the metal bowl of peeled eggs and came to the Bulibasa. They said a few words, and Bulibasa grabbed an egg.

"Bogdaproste," he said, eating it whole.

The girls then went to the next man, and the next, every time saying the same thing, like a mantra.

They skipped Tibi and went to the other fire, where the other men were. And there were just enough eggs for the men to eat one each.

"Come," said Bulibasa, suddenly, as the whole council rose. Tibi followed, blinking often as he tried to snap out of his drowsiness.

They all walked closer to the center of the yard, where Tibi could now see what the little girls had put together.

It was a clay puppet, about two feet long, and each girl seemed to have had a part of it under her care. Four had made the arms and legs, one the body, and another the head.

The six little girls now took pieces of red eggshell and placed them on the puppet, carefully pushing them into the clay. Once they'd each finished their part, the clay puppet was now fully red, except for a long oval on the chest, which had been left bare. The chest looked like a red clam with a muddy interior.

"Give me your blood," said Baba suddenly, startling Tibi, who was mesmerized by the blood-red clay puppet.

"What?" asked Tibi, turning to his right. Baba was there, holding a red chicken chest bone in her left hand and a knife in her right.

"Give me your blood," repeated Baba.

"Oh, okay," said Tibi, staggering as he turned. "Here," he said, pushing his index finger forward, facing up.

"No," said Baba.

"Oh, you want more," said Tibi, taking a wobbly step back. "Whew, that drink, or the smoke, it really got me," he said, laughing a bit, yet no one joined in. "Here, my palm," he said, opening his left palm to Baba.

"No," said Baba once more.

"No? But… what… how can I give you blood then?"

"Chest."

"Oh… Yes, okay," said Tibi, touching his chest as he continued to waddle. "Man, do I mumble when I speak? Or can you—"

"Chest. Now. No time to waste."

"Okay, okay. But don't… I mean, don't stab me, please."

Suddenly, a few men grabbed Tibi's hands, holding them to the sides.

"Hey!" he said, taken by surprise.

Baba came close and ripped open his jacket. With her knife she cut his T-shirt, exposing his chest.

Oddly enough, Tibi didn't feel the cold, and he took a deep breath.

"I'm not scared," he said, talking mostly to himself. "You know what? It must be the alcohol, or the smokes, but— Ow! It hurts!"

Baba was pressing the length of the blade to his chest, right above his heart. As she pressed, blood appeared, large drops taking form. Baba held the chicken bone below the knife and, as blood dripped onto it, she started repeating a few words.

"Blood is given. Bogdaproste. Blood is given. Bogdaproste. Blood is given." Over and over she said it, and soon Tibi started perceiving it as background noise.

Suddenly, she stopped. She turned around, approached the clay puppet, and placed the bone, now covered in both Tibi's blood and the chicken's, on the puppet's chest, the spot not covered by eggshells. She pushed the bone deep inside, repeating those words again.

"Blood is given. Bogdaproste. Blood is given."

She pressed the clay together, making it fully cover the bone.

She rose, and as she continued her incantation, the six little girls grabbed the remaining eggshell and filled in the gap.

Baba then knelt in the mud and slowly removed the puppet from the ground, placing her hands underneath it. She held it carefully, like one would carry a newborn, safeguarding its head and limbs, and slowly moved it to the hole in the ground, while continuing the same incantation, over and over.

Baba got up and the six little girls now buried the puppet, grabbing the cold, moist mud with their bare little hands and patting it down.

At the same time, all the women in the village started wailing and lamenting, like someone had just died. They were crying and yelling, kneeling as large tears raced down their battered cheeks. Some were pulling hair from their heads, or even tearing apart their clothes.

Tibi looked around, still taking deep sips from his pipe, smoking and turning slowly. The world was moving, and the sounds seemed muffled to his intoxicated ears. And while the women were going at it, the men each took another mug of that strange drink, all mumbling a few words.

He got his mug filled and drank it, nodding as he realized that, now, the drink tasted and smelled divine. Time seemed to stretch out.

* * *

After what felt like hours later, the wailing stopped. The little girls grabbed a few boxes and put them over the burial site. On top they placed a few rugs, and then went to the sides, three on the left and three on the right, all facing Baba.

The old crone turned to the girls, who were all now looking at her, waiting. She moved her hand, slowly, and pointed to the oldest girl serving the ritual.

The girl came forth and Baba grabbed her shirt and jacket, ripping them apart. She continued tearing and pulling until the girl stood fully naked.

Baba said a few words and one of the little girls came with a clay flask. The old lady took it, removed the cork, and gave it to the naked girl, who drank it entirely.

During this time, Baba continued her incantation.

"Blood is given. Bogdaproste. Blood is given." Over and over, like a humming.

The naked girl then moved to the boxes. She lay down, face up, and the men now turned toward her, leaving just enough room for Baba to move around.

Two of the girls stepped forward, one holding one of the dead chickens, the other an empty bowl. Baba grabbed the chicken and, with expert moves, cut one chicken leg, handing it to Bulibasa. He took the chicken leg and rubbed it on the naked girl's body, saying the same incantation.

"Blood is given. Bogdaproste. Blood is given," said the Bulibasa, making sure the girl was properly greased with the leg.

He then threw the leg into the bowl. Then Baba went on and cut another piece of the chicken, giving it to another man, who did the same thing.

As the three chickens were finished off, Tibi realized that, yet again, he hadn't received any piece of chicken.

Baba then said a word and the men stood aside, making room for her to get out of the circle and throw the contents of the three bowls into a large cauldron with boiling water, which was set over one of the campfires.

The remaining three little girls came with the three chicken heads on three metal platters. Baba took one and turned toward the naked girl lying on the boxes. Her body was now covered in chicken blood, her skin scraped by some of the pointier bones as they'd moved across her body.

Still, she looked happy, smiling proudly as the men looked down at her with their lost, dizzy eyes, repeating the same incantation over and over again, like a hum.

Baba moved to the burning cauldron.

"Blood links with blood," said Baba, louder, and the 'blood is given' mantra suddenly stopped.

Tibi turned his head to look at her. She was holding one of the chicken heads over the steaming broth.

"Blood links with blood," mumbled the choir of men, making Tibi turn his head now to the naked girl, where the men were gathered.

Baba threw the head into the cauldron. She then went back to the naked girl, where the three girls with platters waited. She picking up another head.

Baba moved back to the cauldron.

"We put it to the ground," said Baba, and the men squatted, touching the ground with their palms. Tibi was looking around, puzzled. Everyone was holding their palms on the ground, pressed into the wet mud.

Tibi realized that everyone was looking straight at him. All the eyes, man, woman or child, were looking right at him, and Baba was waiting, holding the small chicken head up with her right hand.

Tibi squatted, slowly, extended his right palm and touched the ground.

"We put it to the ground," repeated the choir, and Tibi joined in, a few moments later.

Baba threw the head into the cauldron and went back to the naked girl, picked up the third, and last, head, then returned.

"And it rises right back," said Baba louder.

The men rose and turned toward the naked girl. All the men put their muddy palms over her body, waving their fingers and helping pieces of mud to fall over the girl.

Baba approached and, with both hands, spread the dirt all over the little girl's body.

Tibi inched closer as the last men completed their strange, quiet act.

Baba finished spreading the blood and clay and turned toward Tibi.

He looked at his palm, the one he'd used to touch the ground, and saw a few pieces of clay on it. He looked at the girl. She was fully covered in mud and chicken blood, everywhere except her belly, which was almost clean. Baba was holding her dirty palms toward it, pointing at the clean skin, and he took a step closer.

He extended his hand, toward the girl. Yet he stopped, looking around puzzled.

"She's just a girl," he mumbled, his tongue feeling numb, and he instantly saw people throwing him mean looks.

He sighed and moved his hand over the girl, dropping a small piece of clay onto her belly.

"And it rises right back," said the choir, as Baba's hands resumed their movement, spreading the clay on her belly as well, as the girl closed her eyes, smiling.

Tibi took a step back. He felt nauseated. All of a sudden, all that alcohol, the smoking, and maybe the whole ritual added up. He staggered and soon found himself down on all fours, vomiting a dark red liquid.

So red! Must be the strange wine, he thought, before passing out.

6 SOUR CHERRY CAKE

T ibi was finally sitting in his armchair. He was facing the window, and behind that window he could see two very wide flypapers hanging from the roof, swaying slightly as the wind gently caressed them.

There was something strange about those flypapers. When had Mia start using flypaper? And why were they outside the house? Strange, too, that he could see the ugly papers, with Mia usually so careful about how things were displayed.

He changed his position slightly, so he could see between them. It was bright outside: the summer sunlight illuminating the garden.

He could make out plenty of insect shapes, implying that, on the other side of the paper, many were trapped. It was clear they weren't flies. No, they looked like something else, a bit larger. Ah, maybe those black bugs he saw in the Danube Delta a few years ago. The ones that hid inside the sand every time he tried to catch them. Desert beetles, maybe? But were they flying insects?

He suddenly saw the shape of small lizards, also trapped on the paper.

How the hell did lizards get up there? Jesus. And why are we using flypaper to trap lizards?

Tibi rose from his chair, and he found himself walking through a village.

Oh, that's the guesthouse where that room is, he thought, looking to his left. *Horza's place, yes, the dark-brown one. Three Bears. Now that's an original name.*

At that moment, he realized he was carrying two plates. The one in his left hand held four square pieces of sour cherry cake, just like his mother used to make. He could see the sour cherries in it, their red juice slightly spread into the crust. The right-hand plate had only a single piece of the same cake, but it looked old and far less tasty.

Why do I keep carrying this old, rotten thing?

He threw away the right-hand plate and reached for one of the fresh pieces of pie. He took a bite and red liquid spurted out, dribbling down his chin. It was delicious! He took another bite, and then another, finishing up the piece. He took the second piece, and then the third, until he finally lifted the last one from the plate.

As he finished the last bite, someone pulled on his left shoulder and he heard his mother's voice saying, "That was your brother's, you know?"

"What?"

"The pie. Yours was the one you threw away."

"Oh," said Tibi, suddenly realizing that was, indeed, his brother's pie he'd eaten. "I hope he can forgive me."

"He will," said his mother.

"Hey, man." The voice came from his right now, and a bit behind him. Tibi turned, trying to see who it was.

The speaker was a tall man, dressed all in black. He was so close, so in his face, that Tibi could only see his chest.

"What is it?" asked Tibi, continuing to walk.

"You ate me."

"What? What do you mean?" asked Tibi, raising his eyebrows.

"I was one of the beetles."

Tibi suddenly realized the pies weren't really pies. They had been the flypapers that were hanging from the roof, rolled into squares.

"So those weren't sour cherries? Those were beetles?"

"Yes."

"And you were one of those beetles?"

"Yes."

"Oh. I'm sorry I ate you," said Tibi. "I didn't mean to."

"No worries. But there's more."

"What?"

"You also ate my mother."

"What? Really?"

"Yes. She was also there. And she's here with us now."

"Hello, grandson." The cawing voice came from behind the tall, black-clad man.

Tibi instantly recognized the voice and turned hesitantly, his hands shaking. The old gypsy woman, the one with a large dark mole below her left eye, was looking at him, grinning. She was very close to him as well, within arm's reach, a bit behind the tall one.

"Docan is right," she said, continuing to grin. "You ate us. And now we're here with you."

* * *

He woke, shivering. His head hurt and he could barely keep his eyes open. The light was strong and the sun was high in the sky.

His left cheek was cold, and as he tried to move, he realized it was pressed against the wet, mushy ground.

Tibi noticed his right leg was vibrating.

Oh, the phone.

He grabbed the buzzing rectangular object from his pocket with a shaky hand. "Oh, hi Mia."

"Hey! Where are you? What in God's name happened?" Her voice was loud, with a hint of panic.

"Ah… I am… I think I'm back at the campsite. Yes," said Tibi, barely managing to raise his head and look around, as the light was too much for his squinting eyes. He was on his belly, and now he pushed himself up with trembling arms.

"Then why the hell didn't you say anything?" Mia continued to yell through the phone. "See, now you're making me cuss. I was worried sick! You could have texted at least."

"Oh, where are they?" asked Tibi when he finally managed to rise above the ground and look around.

"They? Who? What are you talking about?"

"The gypsies and their campsite. Oh my God, they left?"

The whole clearing was empty, and Tibi was standing there alone, turning around in the spot where he'd slept.

"Tibi! What's going on?"

"I don't know… I mean, I was here, I must have spent the night," he said, looking everywhere, staggering, puzzled, as he moved his gaze around the place. "They did some sort of ritual, I guess. I drank some strange alcohol and smoked together with the Bulibasa. And now, now they're gone."

"Wow, Jesus. It's midday. The next day! How long have you stayed there?"

"I honestly don't know. I don't think it was that late when I lost it," said Tibi, now looking at his chest. "Shit, I slept in the mud."

"What?"

"I don't know how I got here, but I was lying in the mud. I must have lost consciousness some time during the evening, I guess. And it seems I slept until now. Shit," he added, checking for his wallet. "Ah."

"What? What happened?"

"I was just checking my wallet. But it's in my pocket. And I obviously still have my phone, so that's good. They didn't steal from me."

"What happened there? What about that ritual?"

Tibi told her some of the things that had happened.

"Oh, wow," said Mia. "Such a mixture of Christianity and pagan beliefs. Just wow. Why did you get yourself involved in such things? It's bad for your soul, you know?"

"Oh, God, honey," said Tibi, touching his forehead, only to realize it was also covered in mud. "What started this topic? Why do we have to talk about my soul?"

"I know it's not a subject we discuss, but you need to pay attention to these things."

"I guess," said Tibi in a fainter voice.

"Burying clay puppets, taking blood from your chest, with a knife which had been God knows where, drinking smelly concoctions, smoking God knows what. Ah, plus naked children covered in blood. Yes, I know, you just threw some clay on her, but Jesus. You need to be smarter than this."

"I know. You said burying?"

"Yeah. What do you think they were doing? Why were all those women wailing, if not crying for someone who'd died? Haven't you seen on TV how they mourn: crying and yelling that you can hear a mile away?"

"True," said Tibi in an even quieter voice. He was blinking often, forcing himself to regain his focus. His head was still spinning, though, making it difficult.

"Moreover, have you clarified anything? Why were you in that camp in the first place?"

"I was here to… yes, to speak with that old lady. The one with the dark mole under her eye, not the Baba."

"And did you?"

"She wasn't here. I just dreamt about her though."

"Oh, wow, that's just beautiful. Gee, good thing you slept for twelve hours in the mud, after drinking God knows what, only to be able to dream of an old, ugly, strange pagan gypsy!"

"Hey, honey, don't go there," said Tibi, taking a deep breath. "Look, I'm sorry. At least I'm fine. I'll go back to the inn and then, if I'm up to it, I'll come home today."

"It's rather late," said Mia, and her voice gave him the impression she was barely holding back tears. "You should sleep and get some rest. Make the drive tomorrow."

"Hey," said Tibi, bowing his head as he spoke more softly into the phone, "I love you."

"I love you too, you idiot! Why do you think I worry so much?" Mia took a few seconds, and then her voice was calmer. "Just take care of yourself. Go back to the inn, have a shower, eat something warm, sleep it off and come back home."

* * *

Tibi stood there for a few minutes after putting away his phone, taking deep breaths and trying to get a hold on himself.

With sluggish movements, he looked around the clearing. He could see a lot of footprints. Some were barefoot and small, others were large boot prints.

Those little girls are sure growing up differently than I did, he thought, shaking his head.

He turned around, and there, in the middle of the former campsite, he could see a bump in the ground: the place where the mud puppet was buried.

He closed in. It was right in the middle of the clearing and the three spots where the campfires used to be were clearly visible.

My God, this grave is right in the center. Yeah, I guess we should call it a grave. Mia was right: all those women were crying and wailing like someone really had died.

He suddenly remembered the girl lying naked on the three boxes, on top of the grave. He could still see the marks left by the boxes in the mud, but his mind was still stressing about the girl.

I just hope they didn't… No, come on, they couldn't have. She is alive, right?

Tibi shook his head. He could feel a throbbing headache gathering at his temples.

* * *

He was walking by the river, heading back, when his phone started ringing again.

"Hello? Yes? Oh, hi Ana. Yes, yes, I'm fine! No, no need to worry. Yes, I spent the night at the campsite, but all is well. Yes, yes. No need for a secret message," said Tibi, laughing. "I'm free. I'm walking back right now. I'll be there in about an hour and a half. Oh, and you should know that I fell and am fully covered in mud. We'll see at the door how I can enter the Pointy Nose without bringing dirt into the house."

* * *

"Oh my God, Tibi," said Ana, covering her cheeks with both hands. "What happened to you? Are you okay?"

"Yes, yes, I'm fine," said Tibi, smiling briefly as he made eye contact with Ana, then quickly looking down again. "As I said, it was very muddy over there and I fell."

"My God. Fine, let's get you cleaned up. I think you should go around to the back door," said Ana, as a few people walking down the street were casting wary glances at the strange-looking man. "You'll draw less attention that way. People here are curious by nature."

"Yes, yes, got it. Thank you for your help. Really."

He reached the back door and Ana opened it.

"Now, put your jacket down here, on the porch. The same with your boots. The pants are a mess as well. Could you leave them here too?"

"Umm…"

"Come on. I won't look," said Ana, giggling. "Jesus, it looks like you slept in the mud, rather than fell in it."

Tibi smiled awkwardly, and silently executed the orders, while Ana went back inside and then returned with a pitcher filled with water.

"Fine. Now wash your face. You're so muddy. Jesus. Okay. Go inside, wash, and get some fresh clothes. I can help wash your boots, but I can't help with the rest."

"Oh, no, no way you'll wash my boots," said Tibi, shivering as the cold water and wind seeped into his bones. "I'll do it myself. And as for the clothes, if you have a large garbage bag, I will take the rest back home and handle them there."

"Okay, fine," said Ana, with a smile. "See you in thirty minutes. I guess you're hungry, right?"

"Famished."

"That's terrific. I've baked some sour cherry cake. What's with the face? You don't like sour cherry cake?"

"Oh," said Tibi faintly. He then continued, careful to keep his voice light. "No, no. I mean, yes, I like it. I would love some pie."

* * *

"I was thinking of leaving tomorrow," said Tibi, taking the last bite from his sour cherry pie. "Did you really cook this?"

"Yes, I did. Did you like it?"

"I loved it," said Tibi. "You're such a great cook. And thank you for your help today. Really."

"No worries. So, you were saying you want to go? Did you get what you needed from the gypsies?"

"No. Not really, I think. I didn't find the woman I was looking for. But that's that. And, yes, I'll check out tomorrow. I'll pay for the entire stay, of course. No, please," he added quickly when it looked like Ana would protest. "It's Thursday already. It will be difficult to find another person to book Thursday to Saturday."

Ana nodded.

"I want to buy you a drink too," said Tibi, suddenly, "to thank you for your help. I'm in the mood for some wine. Okay with you?"

"Yes, okay," said Ana. "I'll just go check on my husband first. He's supposed to finish trimming some fruit trees."

"No problem," said Tibi. "He's also invited, of course."

* * *

Tibi strode downhill, heading toward the small store. It was almost night, and he was hurrying. His tracksuit, the one he'd brought to wear inside, was not warm enough for the cold temperatures at this time of year.

Too bad my jacket is full of mud, thought Tibi as he picked up the pace. Luckily, he had his warm hat on.

Suddenly, he felt a twinge in his chest, where Baba had cut him with the knife.

I hope I washed it properly and it won't get infected. He took a few more steps, and the twinge increased, becoming more painful. *Damn it,* he thought, touching his chest. *Why the hell did I say yes to that thing?*

The pain sharpened then, making him groan. But after that, it instantly went away, as fast as it had come. He realized he was right at the entrance of the Three Bears guesthouse.

Well, what do you know? Now that's a strange coincidence.

Tibi looked up, toward the windows of Room 26. Nobody seemed to be there, as there were no lights on inside.

Tibi went up the stairs, reaching the guesthouse's main door. After a moment of hesitation, he opened it and entered.

Inside was a group of people, talking. Two adults, a man and a woman, were discussing something with the man at the reception desk.

"So, the return is in the same place?" asked the woman.

"Almost. A few hundred yards away."

It was Emi's high-pitched voice; Tibi could recognize it out of a thousand. He looked around. The lobby was the same as last time he was here and, judging by the number of cars out front and in the small parking area nearby, the place was packed.

The discussion continued. Tibi caught sight of his reflection in the glass pane in the door. He looked down at his clothes. Then he opened the door and got out, heading toward the store.

* * *

"Thank you for the wine," said Mr. Capata, squeezing Tibi's hand.

"It was my pleasure."

"Goodnight," said Ana, as she and her husband left the kitchen.

Tibi went up the stairs and reached his room. He put on his pajamas and called Mia.

"Hey, sweetie," said Tibi, yawning. "How are you?"

"Hey babe," said Mia. "I'm fine. You?"

"I'm sorry I got you so upset before. You sound better now."

"Yeah, well, I've had time to relax. You gave me quite a scare, you know?"

"Yes, I do. And I'm sorry."

"I was really afraid, even though you kept saying it should be fine," she added, her voice breaking down.

"I love you. Please forgive me."

"It's fine. Now, go to bed. Come home tomorrow."

* * *

Tibi woke, startled.

"Damn it," he said out loud. "Now I just changed dreams? And what is it with the beetles and lizards?"

He sat on the side of his bed.

The room was just as welcoming as before, with nothing scary in sight. Still, Tibi was breathing rapidly and he needed a few minutes to relax.

He rose, aiming to go to the toilet, when something made him inch closer to the window and move the drapes to the side instead.

Down there, standing by a lamppost was the old gypsy, the one with a dark mole beneath her left eye. Worse still, she had been present in the dream he just had.

Tibi pulled on his tracksuit pants, grabbed the sweatshirt, and ran out of the room. But by the time he reached the street, just like on the previous occasion, the woman was gone.

"God damn it," he mumbled, going back inside.

* * *

The next morning, he slept until late and then ate the breakfast Ana laid out for him. He had warm, homemade bread with eggplant spread and fresh onions, and once again he had to congratulate Ana on her cooking skills.

He left the inn close to midday.

"Hey honey! How are you?"

"Fine. You're coming home?"

"Yes. I'm driving now."

"So late?"

"Yes. I slept in. It was good."

"That's nice. I'll cook something for lunch. Drive safely."

"Yes, thank you. It's going to be a long ride, I think. The traffic is really bad."

"I guess a lot of people are heading home after Easter. Some came on Monday, but maybe a few took extra days."

"Yeah, I guess so. See you soon!"

* * *

"Hey Mike, how are you?" Tibi was using the hands-free to call his friend.

"Oh, hey man. How's the mission to solve the mystery? We haven't talked in a while. What are you up to?"

"Oh, you're in for a treat. Let me tell you what happened two days ago."

So, Tibi went ahead and told Mike about his day at the campsite, about the ritual and the new dream that seemed to have replaced the old one.

"Oh, man," said Mike. "That sounds horrible."

"Yeah, it was. And the real downside is, I solved nothing."

"Well, I just hope that now, knowing those gypsies are gone, you can finally relax and get on with your life."

Tibi paused for a few seconds, considering Mike's words. "How does that make sense?"

"They left, so you'll never find them again. Why do you think they did it? They did that stupid ritual and then they ran away. So, that's that."

"And?"

"And there's nothing else you can do, that's what I mean. Time to leave this whole thing behind you."

"You're just trying to make me relax," said Tibi, smiling. "And I appreciate it."

"What gave it away?"

"That thing you said. It makes no sense. Anyway, I almost went back to visit Emi and Horza, you know?"

"Really? What did they say?"

"I realized I was dressed in this tracksuit of mine. It's one I usually wear around the house, so it's rather old and beat up. I looked like a hobo, so I changed my mind and left."

"Yeah, with that bald head of yours and the huge beard, I can only imagine," said Mike, laughing heavily through the car's stereo.

"Yeah, yeah, laugh all you want. And I wasn't bald; I had my beanie on. But, come to think of it, that probably made me look even worse."

Mike continued to laugh. "Just imagine if you'd entered the guesthouse and started rambling about gypsies and rituals and how you'd vomited something red so they *must* let you visit Room 26 again."

Tibi joined in the laughter. He'd just passed the city limit and was almost home.

"Anyway," said Tibi a few moments later, "I really felt awkward. But what bothers me is the whole ritual. It was so strange. I wonder what the hell were they trying to achieve."

7 INTERVENTION

One evening after work, a few months later, Tibi unlocked the door and entered his apartment. He took a few steps and dropped his backpack. Then he heard a faint noise coming from the living room.

"Honey? I'm home," he said, taking a few steps forward.

The noise repeated. It was like the sound of fabric rubbing against leather.

"Oh! What are you guys doing here?" he asked as he entered the room.

Mia and Mike were seated at the coffee table.

"Hey babe," said Mia. "We were waiting for you."

"What is this?"

"Sit down," said Mike, waving toward an armchair.

"Is this some sort of lame-ass intervention?" asked Tibi, laughing, as he sat, and Mike immediately joined him.

"Hey!" said Mia, frowning at Mike.

"Ah, yes, sorry. No!" he said, turning back to Tibi. "I mean, yes, it's an intervention. But it's not a lame-ass one!"

"You're not well," said Mia, as Tibi started to turn away. "Please stay."

"Damn it," said Tibi. "I'm fine!"

"You're not fine," said Mia. "Ever since you went alone to find those gypsies, a few months ago, you've been going from bad to

97

worse. At home you're always tired. You watch TV all evening, then go to sleep as late as possible. It's already summer, but you still haven't resumed your exercise routine and—"

"I'm working too much!"

"Not true, man," said Mike. "You're always sleepy at work. The boss seems less patient with you. You come in later than usual and leave sooner. You need to snap out of it."

Tibi listened in numb silence, then shook his head.

"You used to be a happy guy," said Mike. "You know, I could make fun of you and you would make fun of me."

Tibi's reply was gruff. "I'm still a happy person. I just don't like horsing around anymore."

"I can understand that. You know, we all became adults and such. But you're not happy."

"Yes, I am. Okay, I'm not grinning and smiling all the time, but I am." He crossed his arms and stared at the wall.

"Yeah, I do sense massive happiness hidden deep inside. Jesus, please control it, it's contagious," said Mike, overemphasizing the words and grinning. Yet his grin immediately went away when Mia threw him cold glances.

Tibi stayed silent, looking between his wife and his best friend.

"Your desk, much like your house," said Mike, looking around, "used to be the cleanest and tidiest place I've ever seen. But since your mind is so clearly somewhere else, now even that is in disarray." He threw a quick glance at Mia, who was eyeballing him, and tried a friendly grin. "I mean, just his desk. The house looks as wonderful as always."

"Look," said Tibi eventually, in a calm voice. "I'll be frank. I know these interventions rarely work. However, I'm different from other people. It's true I've been hiding some things from you on purpose. I didn't want you to know what was going on. It was a vain attempt to hide my weakness."

"But you must talk to us!" said Mia, leaning forward and grabbing his hands.

"Yes. I know. I didn't want to put pressure on you, or worry you too much. The thing is, you're right. It's worse. The dreams I used to have of walking in the woods and shoveling for something have now been replaced by another dream. And this one is repeating every night. The one with those damn pieces of sour cherry pie."

"Ugh, that's a sick one," said Mike, shaking his head.

"And, more frustrating, every time that old gypsy woman and that tall man, Docan, want to talk to me at the end, I wake up. I have a feeling they want to tell me something. Something important."

"Have you thought," said Mike, "that maybe the tall dude dressed in black—"

"Docan."

"Yes. Have you thought that maybe Docan is somehow connected to the shadow you saw in Room 26, and—"

"Hey, Mike! Jesus!" said Mia, interrupting. "We're here to help him, not to encourage—"

"No, but he's right," said Tibi. "That's what I was saying. Of course, I already thought of that. I believe they're connected. But I didn't tell you anything, because the main conclusion is very strange. I think I am somehow connected to these people. That ritual built a bridge, some sort of link between us. And that Baba, she said some things," Tibi continued, his voice grave and intoning as he said, "Blood links with blood. We put it to the ground and it rises right back."

They all looked at one other in silence.

Tibi gripped the chair arms, digging his fingers into the fabric. "I gave blood to that damn puppet," he said after a few moments. "I linked with them, as in the 'blood links with blood' part. The Baba put the clay puppet into the ground. So, that's the 'we put it to the ground' part. I just don't know what 'and it rises right back' means, and I'm not sure I even wanna go there."

Again, no one said anything. Mia was tapping her chin, looking down with a vacant expression.

"Look," said Mike, shifting in his chair. "What can we do to help?"

"Honestly?"

"Yes!" said Mia. "Please, please be honest! We want to help."

Tibi's voice came out raspy. "I have to get back to that room."

"Oh, God!" said Mia, gazing past him, confused.

"You asked for honesty."

"Yes, but—"

"Let him speak," said Mike, interrupting Mia. "Tell us, Tibi, what is the plan?"

"I have to get back into that room. I want to try the priest thing, the one you proposed, Mia." He paused for a few moments, his eyes moving left and right, as he calculated. "Look. I'm telling you, you can't possibly understand what I'm going through. It's tough not being able to have a good night's sleep. It's horrible to keep having those dreams, those sinister dreams that are always the same."

Mia and Mike looked at each other, then at Tibi.

"Something happened in that room. I can feel it. I mean, it's obvious it did. And it's somehow connected to the old gypsy and to her son, Docan. I would say it's likely that Docan died there."

Mia gasped. "How could you know that? Did you dream about it?"

"What? No, no. There is no proof, if that's what you're asking. But the Docan in my dream is tall, and the shadow I saw is also tall. That old gypsy noticed something when she met me, and then she keeps on popping up at night, standing under lampposts, whenever I go to that resort village. They tell me in my dream that I ate them and now I am connected to them. This is it. Something must have happened to Docan in that room. I need to find out what, and then I think it will all be over."

Mike nodded, throwing Mia a questioning look.

"What if we do the priest service?" she eventually asked. "You said you want to try that."

"Yes. It might be a simpler solution, I guess. A priest might just push away the evil, if we can call it that, or bring peace to those souls or whatnot, and maybe that will be enough."

"Okay," said Mike, "sounds like a plan. But how can you book the room? Remember, Emi and Horza think you're a weird freak. They practically banned you from the guesthouse."

A smile lit up Tibi's face. "That's why you'll get the room for us."

"Hmm," said Mike, nodding and pausing for a few moments. "Okay. But how do I ask for Room 26 without raising suspicions? I mean, besides being the last to the right on that floor, there's nothing special about it. It doesn't have a better view; it's not larger or nicer. Hell, it has only downsides, if you take into consideration it being haunted and all," said Mike, laughing.

"Yeah. But I have a plan. You'll say you want to take the entire floor for the whole weekend. Book all six rooms for Friday to Sunday."

"Wow. Okay. That's going to be expensive as hell."

"I don't care," said Tibi. "If it will help me, I must do it."

"Okay. But keep in mind, they might have reservations. We may have to wait a few weeks to find availability."

"The sooner the better, but it's fine by me to wait. I need access to that room."

"Fine. And then, how do you enter the Three Bears? Remember, Emi is watching like a hawk. And so is Horza."

"I have a plan for that as well," said Tibi, grinning.

Mia still seemed mired in the mud of her worries, but she quietly nodded in acknowledgement.

* * *

The car pulled up at the small Pointy Nose inn just as Ana was coming out of the main entrance.

"Oh, hello," she said, when Tibi got out. "You came too early. The room isn't ready yet. Oh, wow, what a change of look," she added, smiling.

"Yes, well," said Tibi, turning his head left and right for Ana to properly see his haircut, "I shaved my beard, but let my hair grow. It's still short, but I look different, don't I?"

"Yes, you really do," said Ana, moving nearer. "I wouldn't have recognized you if I didn't know the car."

"That's perfect," said Tibi, as Mike and Mia exited the vehicle and joined him. "This is my wife, Mia, and my good friend Mike. Everyone, this is Ana, the owner of this charming little country inn."

They exchanged warm greetings, but then the mood turned serious. "Is there somewhere we can talk?" said Mia, as the pleasantries ended.

* * *

"We might need your help," said Tibi once they were seated at a table inside the small dining room, everyone with a mug of coffee in front of them.

"Sure. What can I do?" asked Ana. She attempted a quick smile, yet she was clearly a little on edge.

"Remember when I went to look for the gypsies a few months ago?"

"Yes," said Ana cautiously.

"Well, they're somehow connected to some dreams I've been having."

"Dreams?" Ana frowned.

"Yes. I'm having some strange dreams and I think—"

"Maybe you should start right back at the beginning?" Mia interrupted.

"Yes, that's probably a better idea," said Tibi after a moment's consideration.

So, as the minutes passed, the three of them brought Ana up to date with everything that had happened over the last four years.

* * *

"Wow," said Ana, shaking her head. "I wouldn't have expected this."

"Well, now you know everything," said Tibi.

"And we want to help him fix this," said Mike, joining in. "It's too much for one person, and he's been fighting this for almost four years now."

"Yeah, I get it. And now that I think of it, I might know that Docan character."

"Really?" asked Tibi.

"Not in person. But I think I saw him around a few times. He was indeed a gypsy, and he came down from their campsite to work in the village. He always had his toolbox with him, which I remember thinking was odd at the time. But what struck me most was his height. That, and the toolbox, is why I can so easily recall him now."

"He could be the guy, yes," said Tibi.

"I mean, I'm not sure he's the one. I never knew his name. But I have seen a very tall gypsy, that's what I'm saying."

"Why was the toolbox odd?" asked Mike.

"Well, I don't think he was an expert or anything. He was doing low-level work, as far as I know, for food and a little money. So, I guess I assumed the ones who hired him should have had all the tools he needed. That's why."

"But a good handyman always carries his tools with him," said Mike. "So I still don't see why it's odd."

"That's what I'm saying. Most of the workers around here are not professionals. They're just people who can do a few jobs around the house or in the garden. They're not necessarily highly skilled or anything. They usually just use the tools they get given at the job site."

"Okay," said Tibi. "So, if he's the one, we need to know what happened to him."

"Okay, got it. What do you need from me?"

"Will you help?" asked Mia, eagerly.

"Yes. I mean, if I can, if it's in my power, I want to help."

"Perfect!" said Tibi, punching the air with his fist. "First off, we need a priest."

"You want to exorcise the room?"

"Yes. How did you know?" asked Mike.

"Why else would you need a priest here? Aren't there thousands in that city of yours?"

"So, can you help?" asked Tibi.

"I think so, yes. I know the priest here. We go to church. We're good Christians."

"Great. Can you maybe talk to him about performing a service this evening? It's Friday, we have the rooms booked at the guesthouse, so we'll go there together and just do it."

* * *

Mike and Mia strode confidently downhill, under the strong summer sun, toward Horza's guesthouse. They reached the Three Bears, looked up at the building for a moment, then entered.

"Oh, hello," said Mike to the person at the counter.

"Hello sir, ma'am. Welcome." The receptionist's voice was very high-pitched.

"I'm Mike. We've exchanged many emails during recent months. I've booked the six rooms on the second floor. Oh, and this is my girlfriend."

Mia remained silent. Sunglasses covered her beautiful blue eyes and she was wearing a flowery dress and a hat. Her outfit was certainly different from her usual jeans and T-shirt: what she'd been wearing the last time Emi saw her.

"Ah, yes, nice to meet you in person. Both of you. I'm Emi. And, yes, of course I remember. So, you have the six rooms for the entire weekend, right? Until Sunday."

"Yes, that's right," said Mike, as Mia continued to stand there, looking at her phone.

"And when are the other guests going to join us?"

"They should arrive later today. They're coming from the train station, just like we did, but they're all taking different trains, coming from different locations, so I'm not sure when exactly they'll arrive."

"I see," said Emi. "Will they need help finding the guesthouse?"

"I don't think so. They're big boys and girls; they can take a cab," said Mike, followed by a chuff of laughter.

"If you need a cab, we have the phone numbers of a few drivers," said Emi. "And if you could instruct me who is to stay in which room, I can direct them to the second floor as they arrive."

"Oh, no bother," said Mike, trying to act friendly yet casual. "They'll manage. And you don't need to worry. I will be in contact with them, and as soon as they arrive, I'll come and greet them. I mean, it's the first and only time we'll be celebrating our engagement, right?" he added, turning to Mia, who just nodded, maintaining a blank expression.

"Great," said Emi. "Then should I give you the keys to all the rooms now, or should I keep them?"

"Give them to me, that's fine," said Mike, grabbing the lot. "Thanks. See you."

"Wait," said Emi, coming out from behind the counter. "I'll come along to show you the rooms."

"Oh, no need," said Mike, waving his hand. "I've seen the pictures on your website. Unless there's something specific you'd like to show me?"

"Nothing, I guess. Have a pleasant stay then," said Emi,

reluctantly going back behind his desk.

* * *

"Jesus," whispered Mia, as they reached the first floor. "I thought he made us. Did you see how he was looking at me?"

"No. I mean, he was staring a bit, but I think you're just projecting your fear. He didn't recognize you. The way I see it, he was simply put off and embarrassed by your beauty."

"Oh, stop it," said Mia, hitting his arm.

"No, I'm not even trying a stupid joke. He seemed to be trying not to look at you. And whenever he did look, I guess he took it as a failure. But enough about that strange fellow. Let's see the rooms," said Mike as they reached the second floor.

"That's the one," said Mia, pointing to the door. "Strange, again, that it's the only one with the door closed. Let's see what's inside."

"No way," said Mike, shaking his head. "I'm not entering that room."

"Come on. I didn't know you believed in these things."

"How can I not? I've seen what's happened to Tibi."

"Yeah, well. All things considered, I still believe it's in his head. But I hope this will fix it. And pay attention," said Mia, turning toward him and pointing her finger. "Don't you act like this when he's around! Just make sure everything is relaxed and friendly, and I hope this weekend will solve everything."

"Yes, ma'am," said Mike, making a tipping-of-the-hat gesture while following Mia into Room 26.

Inside, everything looked normal. The corridor was as she remembered, the yellow wall to the left and that strong red color on all the other walls, to two thirds of the way up. The bathroom door and window were open and a pleasant, mellow breeze was blowing in. They advanced alongside the yellow wall and saw the bedroom to the left. A window there was open, too, the drapes slowly moving, and everything was very bright.

"This looks okay," said Mia, turning around. Immediately, she let out a short yell when she saw a man silhouetted next to the entrance. "Jesus, you scared me!" she said, covering her mouth.

"Oh, sorry," said the man. "I'm Mr. Horza, the owner of this place. I wanted to meet in person the couple who had booked the entire second floor."

"Oh, yes," said Mike, clearing his throat. "I'm Mike and this is my wife to be, aah… Andreea."

"Nice to meet you," said Horza, with a quick fake smile. "How do you find our rooms?"

"Ah, this one is great, yes, very pleasing," said Mike, looking around the room and nodding. "Yes. Really good for us."

"I see. Have you seen the others or have you just started the tour?"

"No. I mean, yes, we just started the tour. This is the first room we've seen."

"Interesting," said Horza, trying another smile, now looking straight at Mia. "You started with the last room."

"Ah, yes," said Mike, laughing briefly. "It was the only one with the door closed, so we thought 'what the hell'? Why would that be closed, you know? Ha! It was the one that was different. But not different-different, more like—"

"I think I've got it," said Horza, now without a muscle moving on his face. "So, I wish you a happy life together, and enjoy your stay."

"Oh, yes, thank you, yes, thank you," said Mike, bowing slightly a few times.

"Jesus," whispered Mia, puffing. "He can be so strange. Did you see how he looked at me?"

"That one really ogled you," said Mike, shaking his head. "I thought we were done for."

"Well, we're not. Let's see the other rooms."

"Which one should I take?" asked Mike, still in a quiet voice. "Damn, I'm worried he might hear us."

"You can choose whatever room you want. Tibi and I will take Room 25, so we can sleep, and we'll go to 26 when needed."

"Okay. Then I'll take Room 21."

"Really? Why that one?"

"It's the farthest from Room 26, of course."

* * *

"I think he's here," said Ana, throwing a quick glance at her phone which had just *dinged*. "Come."

Tibi followed her through the main front door, to where a relatively expensive black sedan had just pulled up outside. A man got out. He was in his fifties, with long, gray hair, a full beard and of average height. He was a bit overweight, and he was wearing long, black Christian Orthodox priesthood vestments.

"God be with you, my children," said the man, making the sign of the cross.

"Father, bless," said Tibi and Ana at the same time. Ana then stepped forward and kissed the priest's right hand.

"May the Lord bless you," said the priest, tracing the sign of the cross on her, with his fingers held in a particular way.

Tibi watched the whole scene from the inn's doorway, and then, not knowing what to do, decided to bow his head toward the priest while looking down. The priest smiled briefly.

Another man, younger, early thirties at most, came quickly from the side of the car. He, too, had a long beard and black clothes, only his hair was darker.

"It's a warm day," said the priest, looking up to the sky. "God is looking down on us and taking care of us."

"Come inside, father," said Ana, making a little bow. "We have some lemonade. Or some wine if you prefer."

"Lemonade will be just fine, child," he added as he took the few steps toward the porch. He grunted a little, as if it were difficult for him to walk, and extending his hand as if asking for support.

Ana jumped quickly to help him.

As they approached Tibi, the priest stopped and turned slightly toward him. "I am Father Ilie from the church in this village. And this is my deacon."

"Hello, father, deacon. I am Tibi. Thank you for coming."

"See here, Tibi," said Ilie, entering the building, making the same small grunts with every step he took, "you need a different… attitude if you want to achieve what we are setting out to achieve. Oh, yes, thank you, Ana, yes. I need to rest my old bones," he added, accompanying his sitting down with the loudest grunt yet.

"I see. It's just that I'm not a strong believer and—"

"Then how can you expect an exorcism to be performed?" Priest

Ilie's eyes were burning, and Tibi needed all his will to be able to hold his gaze. He needed even more to measure his next words.

"I do think that priests can have some sort of divine blessing, one that helps them perform such tasks," he said, talking slower than usual, "without the need for everyone present to be a fervent believer."

"All through the grace of God," said Priest Ilie, nodding, as Ana made the sign of the cross. "I see. Well, if we are to do this, you must participate. I mean, just hearing what you say, at the limit of blasphemy, I would be inclined to say no," he added, turning toward Ana. "Why did you call me if you knew we were dealing with non-believers?"

"The wife is a believer," said Ana, throwing glances at Tibi.

"Look, father," said Tibi, extending his right arm and grabbing Priest Ilie's attention. "We really need your help. I think, no, *we* think a soul got stuck in one of the rooms at the large guesthouse down the road. The dark-brown one, the Three Bears."

"Yes, I know it."

"You're the only one who can make it go away."

"That's what I was saying. I would be inclined to say no, but I cannot say no to casting away the devil."

"The devil?" asked Tibi, looking a bit sideways toward the priest.

"Yes, the devil. You said a soul; I say the devil. And even if it is some poor soul, stuck there on his way to heaven, or to hell for that matter, I still believe it's the devil keeping it from moving forward. So, you see, my child—oh, thank you, Ana, I needed some refreshment. As I was saying, so you see, my child, this is why I believe we should all take part in this with open hearts, and let God perform His miracle through us."

"Okay, father," said Tibi. "I'll do my best. What should I do?"

"For starters, you could make the sign of the cross when appropriate. And if you don't know when, just follow my lead, or the lead of others. Think pure thoughts and let God and the Holy Spirit guide you. You are lucky I received training in exorcism, so you have a priest who can really help."

Tibi said nothing, looking at Priest Ilie and nodding.

"Fine. Now, let's go?" said Ilie. "Ana, lead the way."

* * *

"Father, bless," said an old woman who was going uphill. She stopped and bowed, looking at Priest Ilie as he headed down the street, flanked by Ana, Tibi and the deacon.

"Bless you, child," said Ilie rather fast, making a quick cross sign toward the old woman. He did throw her a quick glance, then he continued to walk, while the woman followed him with her gaze, making a few cross signs while looking at the sky.

They continued to walk, and all the locals they met made sure to properly greet the priest.

"This is it," said Priest Ilie as they stopped in front of the large guesthouse.

"Yes," said Tibi. "A friend is coming down; I just texted him. He's got the key. Let's go in."

The group entered just as Mike came down the stairs.

"Hey idiot, how's it hanging?" said Mike, grinning. "Oh, hello, father," he added, turning a bit red.

"Hello, my child."

"Hello father," came a high-pitched voice. "Father, bless."

"Ah, Emi," said the priest, turning around. "I haven't seen you in church for years."

"I know, father," said Emi, blushing. "I've been busy with—"

"You should never be too busy to come to church. That is the way of the devil. You are busy now, busy tomorrow. Next thing you know you never go into the House of God. And then you start questioning God's existence," he added, turning slightly toward Tibi.

"Right, father. I'll… I'll come."

"You promised under God, my child," said Priest Ilie, turning swiftly to Emi. "Not coming is a sin."

"Yes. Yes, I'll be there this Sunday."

"Good, good. Now, where's the demon?" asked Priest Ilie, turning toward Tibi.

"Demon?" Emi visibly jumped. "What demon?"

"The demon haunting this house, of course," said Priest Ilie, looking up the stairs. "Second floor, isn't it?"

"Ah," said Emi, looking puzzled. "There is no demon…

haunting anything."

"Yes, there is," said Tibi, taking a step forward. "It's in Room 26!"

"Ah… Now I see… You're Mr. Coman, right? I thought it was you. But, no, there's nothing… I'll go call Mr. Horza," said Emi, sprinting behind the stairs.

"What is this?" said Priest Ilie, turning to Tibi. "Is this some sort of a joke?"

"No, father. No, it's not. There really is a demon there, and it needs banishing."

"What's going on?" said Horza, coming out from behind the stairs. "Father Ilie. Ana. What's going on? Emi tells me something about an exorcism."

"There is a soul in Room 26 and we are here to make it go away," said Tibi, grabbing Horza's attention.

"You! Emi told me it was you, but I didn't believe you had the nerve. Father," said Horza, turning to the priest. "He's taking you for a fool. There is no demon in any room in my establishment. Come, let me take you to dinner and let's forget this."

"If there is no demon, then there should be no problem if we just bless the room then, isn't that so?"

Tibi's words made Horza freeze for a few moments. He turned back to the priest, now with an oily tone and his head slightly bowed. "Your holiness, please, let's not indulge some crazy—"

"It's the Church's duty," said Priest Ilie suddenly, now in an official tone, "to fight off the devil in every corner. If there is a demon roaming in that room of yours, I must fight it. And if there isn't, any house could use a blessing at least once a year. So, let's go."

"But what if I tell you that Mr. Coman is not allowed on the premises?" said Horza, looking like he was playing his last card. "He's received an interdiction and we don't want his lot in here."

"With or without me," said Tibi, "you cannot stop the Church from doing its work. I just want to see how you can say 'no' to a representative of the—"

"Mr. Coman," said Priest Ilie in a louder tone, "do not presume to speak for the Church! But, yes," he said, addressing Horza, "I will go and perform my duty. Now, let's go. We're wasting time!"

"I will call the police!" said Horza. "I don't care who you are."

"You think anyone from the local force will stop *me*?" asked Priest Ilie, turning his burning eyes on Horza, who involuntarily took a step back. "I baptized all of them. And if not them, their children. Their parents all come to my church, which is something I cannot say about you. And they are all believers. Do you think they will raise a finger to stop me from banishing the devil or blessing a house?"

"Whatever the answer to that question is," said Horza, fists clench and face reddening, "this is not how it should work. This is my property and I can choose who I let inside. And I don't want you to do any exorcism in here."

"Hey, buddy," said Mike in a tone that showed he was losing his patience. "We've paid for the rooms, for two nights each, and I have all the emails to prove the second floor is booked. Just try not letting us enter and I'll bring the Consumer Protection Office on your ass so hard you'll never know what hit you."

"Why would you be against it?" asked Ana, taking a step forward and trying a more peaceful approach. "We'll just go in and do a sermon. Nothing else. After that, Father Ilie will be on his way. Everybody wins, including your guesthouse, which gets blessed, right?" She paused, and everyone else nodded. "You wouldn't want us to think you actually have something to hide, would you?"

"Fine," said Horza eventually, spitting out the word. "Go. And as for you, Ana, I'll remember—"

"Hey! Don't you take it out on me," said Ana, raising her hands involuntarily. "I'm just helping out some customers. I'm not taking sides. And if you have something to tell me, you can tell it to my husband."

Horza turned and left, retreating back behind the stairs, while Emi stood there, looking awkwardly at the group.

"Finally," said Tibi, climbing the stairs, leading the rest of the group, as night fell over the village.

8 EXORCISM

Tibi opened the door and entered the room. He looked around for a few moments, then turned back and called for the others.

"God bless this house and this room," chanted Priest Ilie, making a few cross signs, the action quickly repeated by the others.

Tibi stared blankly for a few moments, but eventually he followed through, joining in the gesture.

"Let us prepare," said Priest Ilie in a strong voice, glancing over at his deacon.

The deacon set his black bag on the bed and opened it. He took out a gold-embroidered scarf-like cloth and held it up. Priest Ilie made the sign of the cross, took the cloth, kissed it, then unwrapped it and placed it around his neck. It draped over his chest, two long, shiny golden parts hanging from each shoulder.

The deacon then took out a large crucifix and a thick, worn Bible. He held these up as well, and Priest Ilie picked them, making further signs of the cross and kissing the two objects.

Now, the priest had the Bible in his right hand and the crucifix in his left. "Where should we start?" he mumbled, looking around the room.

"Over there, Your Grace?" said the deacon in a honeyed tone, pointing to a place near the balcony door, at the foot of the bed.

"Yes, that will do. Good, come," said Priest Ilie, slowly taking a few steps around the bed. "Children, come. Gather around. Yes, you stay there. Give them candles."

The deacon quickly executed the order. He foraged through the bag and pulled out a few candles, which he shared among the people in the room.

"I wonder if he's going to use a lighter," whispered Tibi to Mike, who then looked like he needed all of his will not to burst into laughter.

The deacon picked up a slightly larger candle and then lit it with a match. He shook out the flame once he was done, and then looked around the room as if trying to find somewhere to dispose of it.

"Are you ready?" asked Priest Ilie, who seemed anchored in place by the weight of the crucifix and Bible.

"Just a moment, Your Grace," said the deacon, throwing the match onto the floor and resuming his foraging through the bag. He pulled out a round silver platter with a golden motif embossed around the edge and placed it on the narrow TV console that was set against the wall. He immediately followed up with a golden cup—some sort of chalice—which he carefully set on the platter. "Oh, could you please…"

Ana rushed to take the large candle from his right hand.

"Thank you," mumbled the deacon. He returned to the bag and took out a worn plastic bottle filled with water. He quickly opened the bottle and poured its content into the cup, murmuring a few words.

"I guess that's the holy water," said Mia to Tibi, close to his ear.

Finally, the deacon produced a sprig of dried basil and put it on the platter, next to the cup.

"Now give… Thank you," he mumbled, taking back the large candle from Ana.

"Our Father, who art in heaven—light the other candles—hallowed be Thy name…"

Priest Ilie started ministering, as the deacon scurried around the cramped room, lighting the candles held by the others.

He then moved to the priest's side and carefully took the Bible from him, holding it open and in the right position for Priest Ilie to read from.

The attendees listened to what the priest was saying and singing, following up with cross signs every now and then.

"…Jesus Christ, our Lord, bless us the sinners for…"

The sermon continued as the minutes passed.

The priest murmured something to his right, and the deacon quickly turned toward the platter. He grabbed it with his right hand, trying to keep it steady, together with the cup filled with holy water, and brought it closer to the priest.

Priest Ilie took the basil and dropped it into the cup.

"Lord, come into this house and bless these walls. Keep us safe and…"

Priest Ilie continued his litany, and after every few words he would shake the sprig of basil vigorously, flicking drops of holy water onto the walls.

"Ah," said Tibi suddenly, touching his chest, and Mia threw a quick glance at him, frowning.

"… keep us healthy within these walls, and…"

Tibi groaned, twitching as he pressed his right hand to his chest.

"What's wrong?" whispered Mia, looking at him again.

Tibi fell to the ground, unconscious.

* * *

He was walking down the street. He had the two plates in his hands. The left one had a scrumptious piece of sour cherry pie, and the right one had an older, dried up piece.

Tibi threw away the plate with the old one and grabbed the fresh pie, taking a bite. As soon as he swallowed, he felt a kick in his chest. *What is that?* He took another bite. That, too, was followed by a kick in his chest. *Damn it. What the hell?*

He finished off the pie. Then he realized there was another on the plate.

He grabbed it and took a bite. The kicking pain struck with every bite, and he groaned as he touched his chest.

What was happening?

He put the pie into his mouth, holding it there like a dog carries its food, and used his now-free right hand to pull up his shirt.

The cut on his chest was red and pulsating.

"You need to continue eating," said Docan suddenly, from

somewhere to his right.

"Yes, I do," said Tibi, grabbing the pie and taking another bite. That made the pain kick up another notch, while the cut got a bit brighter.

He finished the pie and realized yet another piece was on the plate.

He kept on eating, piece after piece, until the pain became unbearable.

"What is this?" he said, turning toward Docan. He could only see his chest, all dressed in black, as he was very tall and very close.

"You haven't found it yet," said the old gypsy, the one with the dark mole under her eye. She was there as well, very close to him. "You need to find it."

"What do I have to find?" asked Tibi, almost yelling as his chest pulsated.

"Don't stop eating," said Docan.

"Yes, I must eat," said Tibi, taking another bite, followed by a groan.

* * *

"He passed out! What's going on?" yelled Mia, squatting near Tibi, who was twitching on the floor.

"…Lord, have mercy. Glory to the Father, and to the Son, and to the Holy Spirit…"

The priest threw his arm in a circular motion, sprinkling more holy water, now onto the wall to his left, where the headboard was. As the drops fell, they seemed to spread like dark watercolor paint over a wet canvas.

Tibi groaned and squirmed, grabbing his chest with both hands. His candle, which had tumbled to the floor when he initially passed out, was still lit.

"Careful with the candle," said Mike suddenly. "It's catching fire!"

The candle set ablaze a corner of the bedsheets, but luckily Mike's stomping was enough to put it out.

"… keep this house protected, and push away the devil who…"

"Aah," groaned Tibi, squirming again as the priest's holy water now sprinkled over the yellow wall.

"It's hurting him!" said Mia, looking at the priest. "Stop!"

"We will not stop," said Priest Ilie in a loud and imposing voice. "We will banish this demon! Our lord, Jesus Christ, bring your love to us. Help us, the sinners, and protect us from…"

"Let's take him outside," said Mike, grabbing Tibi's shoulders. "Come on, help me!"

Mike and Mia started pulling Tibi out, going through the archway into the corridor.

"…You are our savior, we entreat Thine infinite goodness…"

The priest moved his hand around, now flicking drops of holy water all around the room.

"Aaaa!" yelled Tibi, just as a gust of wind swept through the room. He was still on the floor, eyes closed and body twitching.

"Close the windows!" yelled the deacon.

"They are closed!" said Ana, looking around, shaking.

"… demon, leave this place! Leave this world and…"

Another gust of wind hit them, blowing out all the candles in the room.

* * *

"But it hurts!" said Tibi, grabbing yet another piece of pie from his plate.

"You must eat it," said Docan.

"You haven't found it," said the old gypsy.

"Eat it."

"Find it."

"Aaaaah!"

* * *

A rumble started in the room as soon as the candles were extinguished. The room was in darkness, save for a faint light from the lampposts outside, which seeped in through the curtains.

Under the feeble light, the walls, now filled with large black spots, seemed to be alive, small waves moving over their surfaces. Hand shapes seemed to take form on the yellow wall, like someone was pushing from behind a canvas. The black spots were all around, and where drops of holy water had hit the walls, the red, yellow and white paint was turning black.

"Jesus!" yelled Priest Ilie, stopping another splash mid-air. He seemed stunned, looking around the room in disbelief. "I must go," he said a few moments later, raising his hem and sprinting. He shoved past Ana to reach the corridor. Then he stepped over Tibi, charging between Mia and Mike, barely missing them.

"Nice!" yelled Mike, turning his head toward the exit. "You can barely move, right? Hey, deacon, pay attention not to hit us on your way out!"

The deacon was right behind the priest, gripping the golden chalice and platter. He tried to jump over the squirming man on the floor, but ended up stepping on his arm.

"You idiots!" yelled Mike again.

Priest Ilie was already at the door, trying to pull it open, yet a strong wind was blowing inside the room, holding it closed. The rumbling was loud and the whole room was trembling, drowning out the yells of the people cowering inside.

* * *

"Will you eat it?"

"Will you find it?"

"Will you eat it?"

"Will you find it?"

"Find what?" yelled Tibi, taking his millionth bite of the sour cherry pie. Red drops from it flew out as his teeth sank into the cherries, and the chest pain was unbearable.

"Will you find it?" said the old gypsy again, looking at Tibi. She and Docan were close to him, bodies pushing together, her eyes drilling through his head.

"Eat it."

"Will you find it?"

"Yes… yes! Yes! Yes, I will find it!"

* * *

"Ah," said Tibi, groaning as he opened his eyes. He was on the floor in the corridor, and as he regained consciousness, the rumbling stopped.

"Aaah!" yelled Priest Ilie, finally managing to open the door. He sprinted out, closely followed by his deacon.

"How are you, my love?" asked Mia, kissing Tibi as large tears rolled down her cheeks.

"I must find it," said Tibi in a faint voice, shaking his head and coughing.

"Find what, babe?"

"I don't know."

Mike and Ana looked at each other, illuminated by the light coming in from the hallway and through the tall window in the corridor, which, until now, had seemed veiled in darkness. Everyone was sweating and gasping for air, throwing scared glances around the room.

9 THE PILE

I t was midnight. All four of them were sitting around the bed in Room 21. Tibi was sitting propped against the headboard, holding a cup of water, with Mia beside him, while Mike and Ana had pulled the two chairs either side of the bed. Everyone was looking at Tibi.

"What happened?" asked Ana in a shaky voice.

"That damn priest," said Mike. "He got scared and ran away. That's what happened."

"Who cares about the priest?" said Mia. "I have to… I must admit, I think you're right. There's something bad in that room, and you somehow picked it up. Do you know how the room looks right now, after all that holy water was splashed around? It's like a giant box covered in black stains of all shapes and sizes. And that thing is linked to you, so there's nothing we can do to make it go away," said Mia, bursting into tears.

"There must be something," said Mike, shaking his head. "For starters, we can go find that thing."

"What thing?" asked Tibi.

"The one you said you have to find."

"I said that?"

"Oh, come on," said Ana, rising. "This is too much. I want to go home, but now I'm afraid to go alone."

"We'll take you," said Mia. "Thank you again for your help."

119

"No problem. And… and if you need anything else, let me know. But not… I mean, not with… I can't be around for another exorcism."

"No, no," said Tibi, waving his hand. "You've done plenty. We had to try it, and you really helped us. Thank you."

"You're welcome," said Ana, tearing up. "I think I know what to do. It's usually safe out here, but I'll call my husband to pick me up in front of the guesthouse," she added, grabbing her phone.

"Back to it," said Mike. "You honestly don't remember saying that?"

"I remember a dream I had when I fainted during the sermon," said Tibi. "The old gypsy was railing at me about 'finding it', but it wasn't clear what 'it' was. Eventually, I promised I would find it regardless, and then I woke up."

"Damn," said Mike, shaking his head.

"He'll be here in a couple of minutes," said Ana. "Could someone walk me downstairs? I'm a bit—"

"Yes, yes," said Mike. "No worries. I'll take you."

"Ugh, poor baby," said Mia, kissing Tibi once they were alone in the room. "What can we do?"

"I wish I knew what I'm supposed to do," said Tibi, fighting back tears.

"Damn," said Mike as he returned. "Going down the stairs, and especially coming right back up, it's just creepy. It feels so awkward, and I was, believe it or not, afraid. You know, after all that."

"Thanks, buddy," said Tibi, smiling. "Thank you for being here."

"Hey, you know me. You lured me here with the homemade sausages at that restaurant!"

They giggled briefly, then fell silent, thinking.

"That damn priest," said Mike, shaking his head. "I bet he's never even done an exorcism before. You didn't pay him, right?"

"That's not even important," said Tibi. "I would have paid ten times over if he could have fixed it."

"Yeah, me too."

"Okay," said Tibi, suddenly. "You know what? Let's not mope around. We know a few things. There's something in that room, and I am connected to it. I was connected from the beginning, but it

120

was something lighter then. Non-binding, if you will. I think I could have broken the link somehow had we attempted it sooner."

"Maybe a priest could have helped in that moment, like he did with my room." Mia's voice was so quiet they had to strain to hear it.

"Yeah, who knows. Maybe. Maybe even today a better priest could have done it. Or a group of them. I've heard there are sometimes three or even seven for an exorcism, depending on the severity of the issue. But I'm not in the mood to try that again."

"But what if it helps?" said Mia.

"Well, now, after I did that damn ritual with the gypsies, there's no turning back, I guess. I think a strong link has been formed. I mean, during the time Father Ilie was throwing that holy water on the walls, I was dreaming about Docan and the old woman, you know? And they were just like always: coming together, so close to my body, a bit behind me. I could see her face, as she's shorter than me, but I never look up to see Docan's face. He's just dressed in black, very close to me."

"What can we do? How can we help?" asked Mike. "Either way, they clearly want you to find something."

"I know! Look. Let's start from the beginning. I sensed something here. There's no denying it. And then I had those stupid dreams of going into the woods and…" His voice trailed off, just as Mike picked up the thread.

"And you were looking for something! Moreover, you found it. Remember?"

"Yes. I was shoveling, and suddenly I struck something hard. Then I woke up, instantly, every time, a bit scared. You know what?" said Tibi, jumping out of the bed. "I have to go. I have to go find it."

He picked up his phone, pressed a few buttons, then waited.

"Oh, hello Ana. Sorry to bother you… No, no, I'm fine, thank you. I hope you got home safely? Nice, nice. Say hello to—yes, exactly, I needed some help. Do you happen to know a place somewhere here in the woods where people would dump construction materials?"

* * *

"What did she say?" asked Mike as Tibi pulled on his jacket.

"Good thing we have our luggage here," said Tibi, kissing Mia. "There's no need for us to go into that damn room again."

"So? What did Ana say?"

"She said she doesn't know for sure, but her husband said that, when doing renovations, some people have the workers throw the excess materials into the forest on this side of the village. So, basically, somewhere in that direction," he added, pointing toward the small window in the hallway. "And this room is identical to Room 26, but mirrored, and these windows point to the same forest. So I guess that's where I have to go."

"*We* have to go," said Mia.

"Nope," said Tibi. "I won't risk your lives for the shit I got myself in. She said some other things as well."

"Like what?" asked Mia.

"She said there are wolves in these woods, and even bears. Sometimes they come down into the village to forage for food."

"I don't care," said Mike. "I'll grab a huge bat and I'm coming with you."

"Yeah!" Mia agreed.

"Where will you find a bat?"

"These yards are filled with sticks and poles. I'll find one that looks like a club. And if not, I'll yank a plank from the fence and still have something I can use to fight by your side."

"You'll do no such thing. And remember, in my dream I'm always alone."

"What can we do then, to help you?" asked Mia.

"It's past midnight, so I guess there's nothing you can do. Just go to bed and sit by the phone in case I need help."

* * *

Tibi went down the stairs, and Mike was next to him.

"Where the hell is he?" Tibi looked around the reception area, yet no one was there.

"You said he has a room out back."

"Yeah. Let's go," said Tibi, heading straight for the closest door and knocking loudly.

"Yes, yes," came a squeaky voice from inside. "What's happening?"

"We need a shovel," said Tibi.

"What?" said Emi, opening the door. He was blinking, squinting into the light and yawning.

"A shovel."

"I don't have a shovel."

"Of course you do. This is a guesthouse in a mountain village. I bet you have all kind of tools," said Mike, huffing.

"I mean… we might have, but I'd have to ask Hor—"

"Then ask him," said Mike. "Or, better yet, tell me which room he's in and we'll ask him ourselves."

"He doesn't live here. He's got his own house down in the city."

"Then I'll call him."

"No, no," said Emi, surrendering. "Come on. Let me pick up my phone and then I'll find you something."

* * *

"Is that any good?" asked Emi, gesturing into the shed at the back of the guesthouse.

The same lamppost that spread light into the corridor of Room 26 allowed Tibi to make out the vague shape of the tools within the wooden structure. In addition, Emi was holding his phone, with its flashlight turned on, pointed at the open doorway.

"Yes. It's just like in my dream," said Tibi. He pulled out the shovel and weighed it in his hands. "Nice."

"Dream?"

"Yeah. Dream. I keep on dreaming about these things. Now, tell me, where did you throw your building waste following the renovations four years ago?"

"Oh," said Emi, fidgeting. "What… what waste?"

"Come on," said Mike, "don't be like that. We're not the police or the Environmental Guard. We just want to know which way to go."

"I have no… I mean, Mr. Horza always handles those kinds of things," said Emi in a tremulous voice. "I was never the one who—

123

" His flashlight jiggled uncontrollably.

"Okay, fine, don't worry," said Tibi, giving Emi's shoulder a reassuring squeeze. "Thank you for the shovel. Go back inside. We'll be fine."

Emi gripped his phone tighter and ran off.

"Why did you let him off that easily?" asked Mike. "I bet he was talking to Horza. I think he kept texting. And he surely knows about the building materials, don't you think?"

"I don't know. But I'm starting to realize it doesn't matter."

"Why so?"

"I recognize this shovel. I've seen it in my dream. That means I will find the place," said Tibi, grinning.

"I don't know what you've got to grin about, but fine," said Mike. "Are you sure you don't want me to come with?"

"No, no. Go back. Make sure Mia is safe. She's in Room 22, you're in 21, so make sure you run to her if she asks for help, as we discussed. Better yet, maybe you can keep her company while I'm gone."

"Fine, buddy. Take care!" said Mike, hugging Tibi.

* * *

Tibi strode through the woods. It was dark outside, the moonlight barely making its way through the thick branches overhead. He held the shovel in his right hand and his phone, with the flashlight on, in his left.

"This was a dumb idea," he mumbled, though he continued to advance. "This doesn't look like my dream."

He paused and glanced up, but then a loud sound made him flinch.

"Damn it," he said as his phone started ringing. "Yes, honey?"

"Hey babe," said Mia. "We're both here in our room, waiting. How's it going?"

"Fine, I guess. I don't know if I'll find anything. I mean, in my dream it's evening and very windy. Dark clouds should be covering the sky."

"Maybe you should come back?"

"Or maybe it's a good idea I'm trying to do it differently? I mean, just following the dreams might not be the best outcome, right?"

"I don't know. I still believe we should have come with you. Or at least you should have gone during the day."

"We had this discussion already. Come on, try to relax, maybe go to sleep. I'll look around for one hour, then I'll come back."

He closed the call, made sure the flashlight was on, and continued his advance through the woods.

The tall trees were now getting closer together, and he was climbing. Suddenly, he realized there was a trail going up, so he followed that. Wind blew through the trees, making the forest hum with each new gust.

At some point, through the rustling of leaves, he thought he heard a noise, like a broken tree branch, coming from his left. He quickly moved the flashlight, yet nothing was there.

Come on, don't do that, he thought, turning to face forward again. *Focus. There's nothing there.*

The trees started to look familiar, yet something was strange. Tibi took a few more steps until he finally saw an opening ahead of him through the thinning trees.

It was about the size of a basketball court, and in the middle he saw a pile of construction materials. He moved his flashlight around, trying to understand what he was seeing. Yet the light was dim, so he could only guess the parts that were farther away from him. The sky must have clouded over, as there was no moonlight now either.

"You bastards," he mumbled, looking around the place. "Polluting the forests. You didn't have a few Euros to dispose of these things properly, eh?" he added, now in a louder voice.

Again he heard something coming from his left, and he spun the light in that direction.

What the hell? What was that? Was it an animal? Impossible, there are no bright-red animals in these woods. Or are there? Okay, let's look for that thing, whatever it is.

He turned his attention back to the pile and moved around it with slow steps. There were some large pieces of broken drywall, different concrete rocks, and a lot of white and gray materials. Here and there were broken metal profiles, buckets of dried-out paint, plaster, cement and other adhesives, and even some broken tools scattered around. Some looked relatively recent, but most of them were old.

A lot of jerks around here, I guess, thought Tibi, looking around the heap. *Ah, there!* He headed toward a pile a bit to the back, where the scraps looked older than the things out front. It also looked familiar.

He climbed over the pile carefully, each step raising a cloud of white dust which immediately settled on his clothes and his boots.

Still, he advanced relentlessly until he reached the top of the older-looking pile. It was about ten feet wide and had a few long beams on top of it. Tibi turned off his flashlight and grabbed the shovel with both his hands.

It wasn't that cold outside, as it was summer, yet he was happy he'd worn his hoodie. The moon and stars were mostly hidden in the clouds, so he waited a few minutes until his eyes adjusted. Then he set his shovel to the ground, pushing it in.

No, it should be up there, he thought, pulling out the shovel. He looked at it for a few moments, then set it off to the side.

He leaned forward, grabbed one of the long metal profiles, and positioned himself to pull.

Next time I'll take some gloves, he thought, still trying to get into a better position.

"Well, well, well," came a booming voice from behind him.

A flash of cold sweat ran down Tibi's back. He dropped the profile and quickly turned around, only to be blinded by a bright flashlight.

"You nosy little bastard!" said the voice. "You couldn't let this be, could you?"

"Mr. Horza?" asked Tibi, covering his eyes. "Is that you?"

"Does it matter who it is? But yes, it's me. Hop down from there!"

"Emil said you were back home, in the city."

"I was on my way there, yes. Until he texted me that you were going to snoop around in the woods. So, I came back to fix this. No. Don't touch that. Hands off the phone. I have a pistol with me, you know."

"If you kill me, the bullet will tell the police—"

"Ha, ha, ha, you really think someone will ever find the bullet? They'll never find your body. Now, come down from there."

Tibi took a deep breath. "Why are you doing this?" He then added, trying a calmer tone, "What have you—"

"What have I done? Does it matter? The only thing that matters is that you couldn't let it go, that's it. Now come. Quit wasting my time."

"You don't have an alibi. My phone is here with me, and the location is saved by all the tracking the apps usually do. They will never—"

"You know we have bears around here, don't you? And wolves. What if I drop you farther away and then— What was that?" asked Horza suddenly, his flashlight moving to his left.

Tibi's eyes followed Horza's beam, yet he couldn't see anything out of the ordinary. Still, he quickly used this interruption to glance to his right, where his shovel was. All that staring into Horza's flashlight prevented him from seeing clearly in the dark, but he had a vague memory of where he'd set it down. He turned to get it.

"No! What the hell is this?" yelled Horza.

Tibi quickly squatted and grabbed the shovel. He continued to watch Horza, who was about two dozen feet in front of him, at the edge of the pile. His flashlight was pointing into the forest, but some larger piles of construction materials prevented Tibi from seeing what had got Horza so riled up.

Still, Tibi took a quick step, going to his left, trying to put some distance between him and Horza.

Horza fired his pistol.

Tibi turned, looking at him again, just in time to see Horza take two more shots, yelling.

The light coming from Horza's flashlight was moving violently and was revealing his erratic movements.

Inside the shaking beam of the flashlight, something small and red was approaching. It looked like a toddler, running fast.

Horza fired two more shots, taking awkward steps backward, when the red thing jumped onto his face.

"What the hell! Help! Hel—"

His voice was now muffled, like something was covering his mouth. The flashlight was on the ground, pointing toward the exit from the clearing, and Tibi sped in that direction. He had to go around Horza, who was shaking on the ground, groaning violently.

Tibi felt his heart squeezing. What the hell was that thing? He got off the pile and sprinted away. He grabbed his phone and turned on his flashlight, pointing it at Horza as he moved past him.

With a gasp, he stopped a few feet away, looking down at the twitching man. Something red, like a thick toothpaste, was covering Horza's face and entering his mouth. It looked like he was trying to bite it, yet that didn't seem to be doing much good.

Tibi flashed with sweat, frozen in place. That red paste was killing Horza. *What is that thing? An animal? Is it a snake? A giant leech? But it looks like red tar. This cannot be!*

Horza's throat was engorged and it looked like he couldn't breathe. His arms were flailing as he tried to grab and pull out the thick, red paste, but he kept losing his grip on it. His neck bulged and he was gurgling, gasping for air.

His chest, however, was worse. It was swollen and huge, like a pregnant woman's belly.

Suddenly, the sound of cracking bone came from the squirming man, just as the last part of the red paste entered through his mouth. His eyes were teary, staring blankly at the sky.

"Shit!" said Tibi, losing his mind. He sprinted out of the clearing and ran downhill through the forest. He needed all his strength not to yell, and his mind was racing. *What the hell was that? Did my mind just made that up? Was I hallucinating? What was it?*

He ran fast, looking back every few seconds. The forest soon fell silent, yet Horza's groans were burned deep into his mind.

He was halfway to the village when, looking back, he thought he saw the red creature behind him. He felt a violent shock of gooseflesh rippling over his skin, and he sprinted faster.

He was expecting someone, or something, to jump on his back at any moment, yet he reached the village without any other incidents.

He turned around to look back at the forest, now visible under the light from the lamppost behind the Three Bears guesthouse, but he saw nothing coming after him.

Tibi left the shovel next to the shed and then dashed around the building to the front door. Parked out front, he could see a luxury sedan, which hadn't been there when he left.

He tried the front door, but it was locked. He pressed the bell and waited, fidgeting.

* * *

"Oh, Mr. Coman," said Emi, looking at his dirty clothes. "Are you okay?"

"Yes, yes," said Tibi, nodding and throwing glances toward the corner of the guesthouse. "Let me in."

"What… what happened?"

"Nothing. I mean, I found the pile, and then I came back."

"Oh," said Emi, looking behind him. "That's Mr. Horza's car. Is he in there?" he added in his squeaky voice, bending as he tried to see inside the vehicle.

"No! I mean, I don't know. But the car looks empty."

"I see. Okay, come in. It's past two, I guess. Goodnight, Mr. Coman."

"Yes… I mean, yes, goodnight," said Tibi, running up the stairs.

* * *

"Oh, you're back!" said Mia, jumping out of her bed. "How was it?"

"Don't worry. Go to bed," said Tibi, removing his shoes.

"Really?" asked Mia, turning on another light. "Man, you look like hell."

"I'm very dirty, yes," he said, removing his T-shirt.

Mike was sleeping in one of the two flimsy chairs, and Tibi reached out to shake his shoulder. "Mike, wake up, buddy."

"How are you?" asked Mike, yawning. "Wow, you look like shit."

"Yes. He's as white as paper. What happened out there?"

"Nothing! Really. Relax, both of you."

"Fine," said Mike, heading out of the room. "Good night, then. We'll catch up in the morning."

"Yes. Night, man." Tibi turned to Mia. "I'll go take a shower, and I just need some—"

He suddenly stopped, turned around and disappeared back down the corridor.

"What is it?" called Mia.

"Nothing," said Tibi, coming back. "I just wanted to check that I'd locked the door properly. Now, go to sleep."

10 GOING BACK

Tibi was walking down the street. He was holding the two plates with sour cherry pies.

He threw away the plate with the old one and started eating the other. It looked fresh and juicy. He took bite after bite as drops of red sour cherry liquid squirted out of his mouth.

"You ate us," said Docan.

"Oh, sorry about that."

"And you ate my mom."

"I didn't mean it."

* * *

Tibi woke, sweating. It was six am, and he let out a groan as he realized it was, again, just a dream.

"Oh, good morning, my love," said Mia, coming closer to kiss him. "How are— Man, you look beat. Did you get any sleep?"

"Yeah. I mean, a few hours."

"You look worse than ever."

"I feel worse than ever," said Tibi, trying a quick smile.

"There's nothing to joke about," said Mia, frowning. "Did you have that dream again?"

"Oh, you mean the one where I eat sour cherry pie and Docan and the old gypsy crone tell me I ate *them*? Yeah, I did."

131

"Hey, no need to get like that." Her tone was curt.

"Sorry, honey," said Tibi. "I'm just tired. But I have to check something."

"What is it?"

"We have to go to the place where the gypsies used to have their campsite."

"Why? Didn't you say they'd moved?"

"That was a few months ago. What if they came back?"

"Okay. And what if they *are* there?"

"I will ask them to break that spell or whatever they did."

"You don't belie—"

"Come on! You saw what happened in that room!"

"Yes, yes. I saw it. But I mean… I don't know what I mean anymore," said Mia, bursting into tears.

"Oh, honey," said Tibi, grabbing her shoulders. "I'm so sorry for all of this. Really. It's my fault. I shouldn't have gone to those damn witches! But what's done is done, and I have to fix this."

"Okay, fine," said Mia, wiping her eyes.

"I love you. You know that, don't you?"

"Yeah, I do. Okay. I'll go brush my teeth. I'll be ready in ten, and then we can go find that camp."

* * *

"Hey, wake up!" said Tibi, knocking violently on the door.

"What?" came a muffled voice from inside the room.

"Wake up, you idiot. We need to go!"

"Jesus," said Mike, as he opened the door. "What the hell is wrong with you? It's way too early."

"We need to go. Now. We have a long day ahead of us."

"Where to?"

"To the gypsy encampment."

* * *

"You did say Ana makes a mean breakfast," said Mia as they approached the Pointy Nose.

"Yeah. Why? You want to sample it?" asked Tibi, as Mike

132

dawdled behind them, yawning violently.

"Yup. We'll go up the mountain, right? So we need energy."

"Sounds fair. Okay, let's go in. She should be up by now."

* * *

"What? You're going to the gypsies again? Haven't you had enough?" asked Ana, stopping in the middle of the small dining room with the plates in her hand.

"I need to get to the bottom of this."

"You're crazy," said Ana, setting the plates in front of her three guests.

"Delicious-looking eggs," said Mike, checking his plate and sniffing appreciatively. "Hey, do you have some bread?"

"Yeah, I do. I made it myself this morning," said Ana. "Right away."

"Mm," said Mike, groaning with pleasure as he took a bite of the fresh bread. "You should sell these."

"I'll call my brother-in-law, Julian," said Ana. "He'll send some policemen with you."

"No, no," said Tibi. "That won't be necessary. Really. We'll go, talk to them, and then come back."

"Ah, but you said they're not there anymore."

"Yeah, I know," said Tibi. "But there's something I'd like to check at their former campsite, so I have to go there either way. And then, yes, I need to find them."

"But my brother-in-law can help with that. I could give you his phone number. Tell him I asked him to help you."

"Yes, please," said Tibi, pulling out his phone.

* * *

A few hours later, they reached the clearing where the campsite used to be. Now, it was empty, just like that Tuesday after Easter.

"Damn," said Tibi. "I almost hoped we'd find them here."

"This is too much," said Mike, wheezing and breathing heavily. "I never signed up for this."

"Walking is good for you."

133

"I guess, but this is mountaineering. I should—"

"Guys, stop bickering," said Mia, as she took a few steps into the clearing. "Let's look around, see if we can learn anything, then go back."

"Yeah, sorry," said Mike. "Go ahead. I need a moment."

Tibi and Mia advanced to the place where the gypsy camp used to be. Mia was looking around, yet Tibi had his eyes fixed on the center of the yard, where a small, excavated grave stood open.

* * *

"What's wrong with him?" asked Mike, a few dozen minutes later.

"I don't know. Babe? Are you okay?" asked Mia.

Tibi was squatting by the small open grave, looking inside it.

"He's not hearing us," said Mike.

"Looks like it. Hey, Tibi!" said Mia, louder.

Tibi continued to stare at the ground. He suddenly extended his right arm, touching the little mound that was next to the grave.

"It's just a hole in the ground," said Mike. "Gee, if you want, we can take some pictures." He paused for a while, grinning. As no one said anything, he continued. "Tell you what, if you answer me, I'll take a picture of the hole, print it and frame it. How 'bout that?"

"It came from here," said Tibi eventually.

"He speaks!" said Mike, putting his hands together as if in silent prayer.

"What came from here?" asked Mia, coming closer.

"The clay puppet."

"Oh," said Mike, his grin suddenly morphing into a scared look. "Damn. I don't like this. Let's get the hell—"

"Don't you get it?" said Tibi, turning to them.

"No, not really," said Mike, and both he and Mia shook their heads.

"It came from here. And then I saw it last night in the woods."

"What the hell? You saw the clay puppet? Where was it?" asked Mia.

"It was by the construction waste pile."

"Who put it there?" asked Mike.

134

"No one put it there. It was moving; it looked alive. And I think it killed Horza."

Mia gasped, taking a step backward, away from the hole in the ground, while Mike let out a few swear words, looking around rapidly.

"Hey, relax," said Tibi, rising.

"How in God's name can we relax?" snapped Mia. "You just said a clay puppet, a *clay* puppet, is moving around and killing people?"

"No. I mean, yes, that's what I'm saying. But you should relax. I think it wanted to help me."

"How… and why… I mean…" said Mike. "You said Horza? Why was he there?"

"He tried to kill me. He had a gun pointed at me. He said I shouldn't have meddled. And then this… thing attacked him."

"Jesus Christ almighty," said Mia, touching her temples with both hands as she staggered away a few steps.

"He had a gun. Don't you get it? I'm really onto something here. He said I should have stayed out of it, or something like that. So, clearly, there is something there, at the dump site."

"Jesus," said Mike. "But the clay puppet. You probably saw something else. It must have been a wolf, right? Wolves look like clay. They are gray, and it was dark."

"No, no. That one was red. Red like blood."

"But you said it was clay."

"Yes."

"What fresh hell is this?" said Mike, puffing and waving his hands to the side.

"It was red clay."

"Ah. And you saw it moving?"

"Not in so many words."

"Meaning?" asked Mike, looking like he was about to lose his temper.

"Meaning it was dark and the flashlight was moving all around. I caught glimpses of something that looked like a red clay puppet, moving fast. I had only split seconds to see it at first. However, I could properly see it when it was entering Horza's mouth."

"Jesus," mumbled Mia, suddenly dropping to her knees and

vomiting.

"Oh," said Tibi, running to her. "Are you okay? There, let me hold your hair."

"Let me be," said Mia in a hoarse voice, spitting and pushing him away. "Go away."

Tibi took a few steps backward and then returned to the side of the grave. "And it adds up," he said a moment later. "It was inside. When I left, I mean, a few months ago. The grave was covered. And now it's open. I think last night it was following me. That means it got out, or it was helped to get out."

"Oh, Lord!" said Mike, looking at the trees. The sun was up and visibility was perfect, yet he kept moving around, squinting at the tree line.

"Stop it. I told you, it helped me. I wonder if I can tell if it got out by itself," said Tibi, squatting again near the little grave.

"You can't," said Mike. "It's too old. Look, it's rained a few times too. It just looks like a hole in the ground with an old dirt pile next to it. Hmm, but this is strange."

"What is?" asked Tibi, rising.

"All around, grass is growing. See? Only here, where the grave is, there's none. It's just dried mud."

"Yeah. That's strange indeed."

"Tell us what happened at the pile," said Mia, who was still a few steps away. "We deserve to know."

So, Tibi told them everything that had happened the previous night.

* * *

Mike approached Mia, who was sitting on the ground, looking down. She seemed lost in her thoughts.

"Hey," he said, sitting by her with a groan. "Damn, it's difficult to sit on the ground."

Mia said nothing and continued to stare down, as Tibi settled on a rock on the opposite side of the clearing, a few dozen feet from them. He also seemed to be deeply introspective.

"Look," whispered Mike. "I've had a thought. I mean, you see how Tibi's became… He's talking nonsense. He's tired and—"

ROOM 26

"What are you trying to tell me?" asked Mia in a coarse whisper.
Mike looked like he was trying to find his words.
"Come on! Spit it out. What are you trying to tell me?"
"What if he's the one who killed Horza?"
Mia said nothing. She just remained there, looking stunned.
"Look, I'm not trying to talk behind his back. God knows I love
him. He's my best friend, and he'll always be. But all that nonsense
with a little clay boy that killed Horza? And look at him now, how
messed up he is. What if he's losing it?"
Mia took a deep breath and started gazing at a point in the
distance. When she finally spoke a few minutes later her voice was
a dull monotone. "We all saw what happened in that room, when
Father Ilie tried to perform the exorcism. No, that was real. As
much as I believe God is all around and He protects us, I think the
devil is also hard at work."
"But a moving clay puppet? And it must have been dark as the
grave in the woods. I mean, that's too much. But, okay, let's hope
it's that. It just sounds so unbelievable. I've seen movies and heard
my fair share of haunted houses stories, but live clay puppets…"
"I know what you mean," said Mia, sighing. "But I know, deep
in my heart, that Tibi is a good man."
"He is. But choking on a clay creature? What if it's just his mind
wrapping around something horrible that he did out there?"
"Stop it," whispered Mia. "I hear you. But hear me too. We need
to give him support. If we see any solid proof that he's to blame, I'll
be the first one to call in the authorities."
"And what do we do about Horza?" whispered Mike, as Tibi
rose again and started moving around the campsite. "Do we call the
police?"
"I don't know. Let's see what Tibi wants. Hey, Tibi! Come here."
"What?" said Tibi as he approached the group.
"What do we do about Horza? Do we call the police?"
"I don't think that's a good idea, Mia, not right now," said Tibi,
after a few moments of thinking. "If he's dead, then that's it.
Nothing anyone can do. And I still want help from the police to
find the gypsies."
"But shouldn't we call it in?" asked Mike.
"Eventually, but I don't see why right now. I went into the

137

woods alone and no one knows he followed me. Let's wait, please. If they come in now, I will never be able to finish what I've started."

"Why?"

"Because if I call, I'll be the first one they question. Then I'll have to admit that I'm the last one who saw Horza alive. And how much water do you think it will hold when I tell them that 'a red clay puppet suffocated him'?"

"Right," said Mike, nodding as he cast a quick glance at Mia.

"We need to clarify a few things first, to find solid proof that Horza was there for a foul reason. So we need to figure this out."

"And what if he's alive?" asked Mike.

"If he's alive and it was just a dream, then he's already safe. No need to call the police. I mean, he either returned to his car or he called an ambulance. He had his phone with him."

Mike said nothing, yet he threw another glance at Mia.

"Anyway, no matter his whereabouts, after we solve it, we'll have to call it in, I think," said Tibi. "Emi poses a danger too."

"What? In what way?" asked Mike.

"Oh, nothing violent. Just that he could prevent me from solving this before I get the police on my ass."

"My God," said Mia, a tear rolling down her cheek.

"This 'police on my ass' sounds so different from your usual self," said Mike, shaking his head.

"Sorry, but it's true. Emi might suspect that Horza went into the woods. And he saw me all covered in dust. Not to mention he gave me a shovel and all that. So, he might make the connection as soon as Horza fails to answer enough phone calls. He could call the police, so I may only have a few more hours in which to do anything. Come on, let's go. The clock is ticking. Actually, let me call Ana's brother-in-law."

Tibi grabbed his phone.

"Oh, hello, Officer Julian Capata? Hi, I'm Tibi. Ana gave me your number. Yes, yes, your sister-in-law. Yes, exactly. Now, I need some quick help, if that's possible. I'm trying to locate those nomadic gypsies that were in this… Yes, those ones. Yes. I'm at their former campsite, but they're not here anymore. Do you have any idea where they moved? Oh… okay. Could you ask the police from the neighboring villages? If they moved somewhere around here, in this county, maybe they know. Yes, thank you very much! I appreciate it."

Tibi put down his phone.

"So?" asked Mike.

"He'll ask around and let me know."

"Great," said Mia, wrinkling her nose. "Now, I guess we'll go to meet the gypsies."

11 SNOWDROP

The phone rang just as they were leaving the small river, heading back toward the cable cars station. Tibi grabbed it with shaky hands and answered.

"Yes? Oh, hi officer! Yes, yes, it's a good time. Oh! That's great news! Thank you very much! Ah, can you do that? Yes, that would help. Umm, I guess we'll be there in about an hour. We're just heading back to the village. Yeah, we're returning from their previous location, but we're almost there. Yes, thank you very much!"

He ended the call and then turned, grinning, to the others. "We did it!"

* * *

During his phone call with the policeman, Mia watched Tibi. As he went on, Mike moved closer and leaned toward her.

"He looks so different," he whispered. "See how white he is."

"He looks sick," she said, sighing.

"What the hell can we do?"

"I think we need to get to the bottom of this. One way or another, he needs some closure."

* * *

"What happened?" asked Mia, as the call ended. "What did he say?"

"He's found the gypsies. They've moved their encampment around a few times since they left this place, but now they've settled a few villages away, farther up the mountain. It shouldn't be more than a thirty-minute drive to get there."

"You want to go to the campsite?"

"No, no. He said the local police have offered to help. The one who sells flowers hangs out around a monument, and they can hold her for a while."

"What? Hold her?" asked Mia. "Why? What did she do?"

"Nothing, nothing. They'll just keep her there until we arrive."

"But that's illegal."

"Yeah, tell me about it," said Tibi. "They can't legally do it, but they will."

"I think they can do it legally, if they wish," said Mike. "She's selling flowers without a permit. I bet she doesn't have a permit, since most of the nomadic gypsies don't even have IDs to begin with. Still, Mia is right. They wouldn't normally detain old ladies who sell a few flowers to make enough money to buy soup. Yet, they would do it if it's a gypsy."

"Yeah, and that's not fair!" said Mia once more.

"Yes, I know," said Tibi, nodding. "And I agree. Gypsies, especially nomadic ones, are generally not well treated. And eastern Europe has its fair share of them. I just hope they treat her right, and the sooner we get there, the better."

"We shouldn't be doing this," said Mia, shaking her head.

"I know. But what else we can do?"

"They could just tail her."

"And if she tries to leave?"

"Then they can stop her," said Mia.

"But it's kind of the same thing, don't you think?"

"Fine, it is," said Mia a few moments later, crossing her arms and frowning. "But it's not fair, and I don't like it."

"Eh, if you want to get into arguments about fairness," said Mike, "it's not fair to the flower stores either. I mean, they are paying taxes and all that, while others sell flowers without the simplest permit."

"I'm saying it's not fair to detain her just so that we can talk to her. If you want to arrest her, just do it. But this is not okay."

"I don't think there is anything else we can do," said Tibi. "I'm sorry, but we need to solve this."

* * *

It was around three pm when the car pulled up in front of a monastery. Many people were entering and exiting the premises, moving through the large interior gardens up to a wooden church, and out to the back of the courtyard.

"Wow," said Mike, "so many people go to church these days. And so close to evening."

"Pfft," said Mia, scoffing. "It's an old monument—a 600-year-old wooden church. It's one of the oldest, if not *the* oldest, Orthodox churches around here. They're just visiting."

"Ah," said Mike, grinning. "I don't know anything about churches."

"I can see that," said Mia, giggling.

"Come on, stop it," said Tibi, pulling ahead. "I see those cops. Let's go talk to them."

"He's no fun," Mike said to Mia.

"Hello, officers," said Tibi, reaching two policemen who were squinting against the glare of the sun. "It's good to stay in shade on such a hot day, isn't it?" asked Tibi, glancing up at the large tree near the bench where the policemen sat.

"You reckon?" asked the older one. He looked almost forty. He was bony, with dark skin—maybe even darker than Tibi's—and he had a large nose.

Unsure how to respond, Tibi attempted a smile. "Anyway… I've been talking with Officer—"

"We know who you are," said the young one. He looked like he was fresh out of the academy, and he seemed to be trying to find a comfortable spot on the bench. "You're the one who wants that damn gypsy."

"Hey," said Mia, taking a step forward, "there's no reason—"

Tibi raised his right hand to cut her off and threw her a warning glance. "Yes, we are. We just want to talk to her, nothing more."

The older policeman assessed the group for a moment, seeming to ponder what to do next. "Well, what are you waiting for?" he said at last, turning to his colleague. "Show the gentlemen to the car."

The young officer got up and trudged toward a beat-up police car parked a few dozen feet away, under another tree.

"They left her inside in this heat," Mia whispered to Tibi as they followed.

Mike lagged behind, dragging his feet and looking back and forth between the two policemen.

"Yeah, I know," said Tibi. "They're idiots. But let's not blow this."

"Pfft!"

"Hey!" yelled the older policeman, from the bench. "The car has two doors to the back."

The young one stopped and turned around. "What... what do you mean?"

"I mean, don't open *that* door," said the policeman in a slow, superior tone. "Go around the car and open the other one. Let our guests in through the other side."

The young policeman followed through on the orders and approached the other side. There, sitting on the curb, were the three little children Tibi and Mia already knew.

"Man, these are her children," whispered Mia into Tibi's ear. "They've been here all this time, watching their mother sit in a police vehicle for hours?"

"Jesus," mumbled Tibi.

"Hey!" said the young policeman, opening the door and turning to Mia and Tibi. "You want to go in?"

"Mister police office," said the young gypsy, who was leaning toward the open door. "Why am I arrested? Can I get out and—"

"Hey!" yelled the young policeman, turning. "Shut it! Go back to that side."

"But my children, they are hungry! Look at them—"

"Go back there! Now!" He then turned again to Mia and Tibi, talking in a normal tone as the gypsy moved back to the right-hand side of the backseat. "Go on in."

"I'll go first," said Mia, entering, and Tibi followed. "Man, it's so hot in here."

"I can leave the door open," said the policeman. The windows up front were already open wide, but his proposal was immediately and gratefully accepted by everyone.

"So," said Mia, trying to smile at the young gypsy woman, who was looking forward, not facing them. "I'm Mia, and this is my husband, Tibi. We met a few months ago, around Easter, remember?"

The woman said nothing, and she continued to look forward.

"Look, I'm… I'm sorry they did this. We just asked them to tell us where we could find you," said Mia in the same friendly tone. "We just wanted to talk to you, that's all."

The woman continued to wordlessly stare through the windshield.

"We didn't want to hurt you or your children. I'm so sorry about this, but we're really desperate," said Mia, suddenly bursting into tears. "My husband, something happened to him. And… and I want to help him. I want to help him get well. And I think you can help. So, I'm begging you, please, help us."

* * *

Meanwhile, Mike was midway between the older policeman and the police car. He continued his slow approach as the young one strode past him, heading back to the bench.

"She stinks like hell," said the young policeman, his nose wrinkled with distaste.

"Yeah," said Mike, with a quick, polite smile. "Jerk," he mumbled to himself.

He approached the open door and leaned in, trying to hear what was being discussed inside. He arrived just as Mia started crying.

* * *

The gypsy finally turned to the left, where Mia sat crying. She had beautiful black eyes and her hair was dark and long, framing her face. She appraised Mia and Tibi for a moment, then finally spoke.

"I am Snowdrop," said the gypsy in a faint voice.

"What?" asked Mia, wiping her tears.

"I said, I am Snowdrop."

"That's your name?"

"Yes."

"What a beautiful name," said Mia, showing her delightful smile.

"Thank you," said Snowdrop, in the same quiet voice.

"Thank you for doing this," said Mia, turning slightly toward Tibi.

"Yes, thank you," said Tibi. "We've met a few times—last time in your previous encampment. I'd like to ask you a few things, if I may."

"Yes. What?"

"First, what was the meaning of that ritual, you know, with Baba and those chickens?"

* * *

"Hey, hurry up!" yelled the older policeman. "We might need that car."

Mike rose and looked back toward the two men. "Sorry?"

"I said, hurry up! We don't have all day to sit around waiting for you. Plus, junior here says you're stinking up our vehicle."

"Should they get out then?" Mike yelled back. A few pilgrims were passing by, entering and exiting the old wooden church, yet none of them paid any attention to the exchange.

"But if they get out, what's stopping that stinky gypsy from running?" asked the older police officer. "And I won't go chasing her. Will you, young one?" he asked his colleague, grinning.

"No way," said the other policeman, as loudly as his colleague. "And if *you* try to stop her, well, that's illegal. Only we can arrest people."

"Just a sec!" Mike yelled back at them. He then leaned down, toward the people in the back of the police car. "I'll go take care of this. I'll try to buy you as much time as possible."

"Thank you," said Mia, as Mike moved away.

"Hey, guys," he said, approaching the policemen, "are you thirsty?"

"Of course we are," said the old one, while the young one

grinned. "And we're hungry too. Hey, stop your grinning," he added as they rose. "There's a restaurant right around the corner," he said, pointing. "They do a mean barbeque. But, you know, I can eat a lot. And drink."

"Don't worry. I'll take care of it," said Mike, forcing himself to smile as he followed the two policemen in the direction of the restaurant.

"I can't drink too much," said the young one. "What if we have to drive?"

"Ugh, these young ones," said the old policeman, shaking his head. "They're all made of milk." He then turned toward his colleague and started lecturing him. "Look at me! I'm doing great. A beer or two during a hot summer day is like drinking water. With this scorching sun, you'll sweat them out in half an hour. Have you ever seen me unable to solve an issue, even after a few beers? Especially involving those pesky gypsies?"

"No."

"Damn right no. I just wonder why the hell they set their camp around our village, that's what I'd like to know," said the old policeman, turning toward Mike. "Why did they come to my village, to disturb our peace?" he added as they entered the tavern.

"No idea," said Mike, looking around the dive in which he found himself. "You said they serve barbeque?"

"Yeah, the best in our village!" said the policeman. "Hey, Tony, bring us three beers on tap. Cold ones!"

* * *

"What do you want to know about the ritual?" asked Snowdrop.

"First, what was its purpose?" asked Tibi.

"It was to link you to the… to Docan and Regina," said Snowdrop. She spoke well, yet with an accent.

"Who is Regina?"

"Regina is the old woman you were asking me about."

"The one with the dark mole under her eye?"

"Yes, that's the one. That's Regina."

"Okay, got it," said Tibi, nodding. "So, it linked me with them. How can I undo this link?"

"Oh, you can't," said Snowdrop, shaking her head.

"What? Never? There is nothing I can do?"

"Oh, it can be broken, but only after completing your part of the ritual. Oh, or it can be broken before the blood boy is born."

"What?" asked Mia, interrupting them. "I understand nothing. Can we start at the beginning?"

Snowdrop looked at her, waiting.

"I mean, Tibi, can you start in chronological order? Perhaps when we first met Regina?"

"Okay. Fine. So, about Regina. When she saw me for the first time, she acted like she saw something strange in me."

"Yes, I guess she did. She probably saw the omen."

"What omen? How could she see anything?"

"Back then, she was the Baba of our village. She could see that."

"And where is Regina now? Can I talk to her? If she is Baba, maybe she can undo that binding."

"Oh, no," said Snowdrop, laughing and showing her gray teeth. "She is not with us anymore."

"Where did she go?"

"She is dead."

"But... when did she die?"

"Oh, about two or three years ago."

Tibi gasped. "What? Impossible! I've seen her around the village, outside the rooms I was in."

"You probably did." Snowdrop nodded. "She was a Baba. She can come back if she wants to."

"Did you ever see her?" asked Mia, grabbing everyone's attention.

"Oh, no. She only appears to people that she wants to, or that need her. Or, in your case, that she's linked to."

"But she wasn't linked back then," said Tibi.

"She wasn't. But she was somehow connected to you."

"Okay," said Tibi, shaking his head. "This is complicated."

"But it's true," said Snowdrop, this time with more enthusiasm. "The Baba is very powerful. She can perform powerful spells, can protect people, can cast curses, can bring luck in your path. She can even link souls and blood."

"Yeah, that part I saw," said Tibi. "Okay, that's getting... That's odd," he said, looking at Mia. "So, every time I saw Regina, she wasn't actually there?"

"Oh, but she was!" said Snowdrop. "I've told you, she was Baba. Now we have a new Baba, but when Regina died she kept on watching over us. All Babas do."

"Okay, but what happened in that room?" asked Mia. "Why does Tibi have that omen?"

"Baba never talked too much about that," said Snowdrop.

"Baba? You mean Regina?"

"Yes, Regina. Ever since I was born, she was Baba of our community, so I never called her Regina."

"No worries," said Mia, smiling. "Go on."

"So, Regina didn't talk too much about that. But she believed her Docan was killed while working in the village for one of those rich people. He helped with building and renovating houses, and somewhere something happened."

"Probably in Room 26," said Tibi.

"Yes. She did say, after seeing you, that it might have happened at the Three Bears."

"But if she's so powerful," said Mia, "why wasn't she already aware of what happened and where? Why wasn't she all over that guesthouse, calling the police and... You know what I mean," added Mia, as Snowdrop gave a sad smile.

"She tried. She went door to door, asking about her son. And after a few minutes, the police came. They arrested her, took her to the police station. They eventually let her go. We could go into the village, but she could only stay at the cable car station. If she came closer, they would pick her up."

"But she was the mighty Baba," said Tibi. "Why was she selling flowers? Why didn't she send someone else to do it?"

"She wanted to learn about Docan."

"Okay, but when she saw me, why did she run away? She saw my omen, so what the hell?"

"Hey!" said Mia, looking at him.

"That I don't know. She probably didn't know it was related to Docan. She just saw a bad omen and didn't want to have anything to do—"

"But she's the Baba!" said Tibi, interrupting. "Why didn't she want to help?"

"It's difficult on the Baba, I think. There are stories in my family about that. How some Babas have lost their minds trying to fight the omen. And we are a… I don't know how to say."

"Just describe it."

"We don't like to mingle with others," said Snowdrop eventually. "She probably wanted to stay out of it."

"Fine." Tibi surrendered, looking a bit lost.

"Okay," said Mia, "but what about that omen? How did he get it? And why?"

"How, I don't know. And I'm no Baba to know why. I only know everything goes through blood."

"Can I get a straight answer?" asked Tibi, seeming to lose his patience and receiving a quick scowl from Mia.

"I'm just saying what Babas are saying. That connections like this only work when the blood is the same."

"What's that supposed to mean?" asked Tibi, while Mia placed a steadying hand on his back.

"It means you are same blood as we are."

"What? How can I be same blood?" asked Tibi, looking puzzled.

"He's not a gypsy," said Mia, smiling briefly.

"Oh, yes, he is," said Snowdrop. "He must have some gypsy blood. Otherwise, it doesn't work."

"What doesn't work?" asked Tibi and Mia at the same time.

"The omen, the connection you got with Docan. And, more importantly, the ritual."

Tibi and Mia looked at each other.

"I have no idea…" said Tibi, trailing off.

"Do you remember your grandparents, maybe?" asked Mia.

"My father is darker, yes, as I am," said Tibi, "but I always thought it was just, you know, a darker shade of Caucasian."

"In the end, it's not important," said Mia, shaking her head. "What next?"

"So, we know I connected with Docan somehow. Something happened to him in that room, now I'm certain of it, and I think I know where his body is."

"You need that, in order to finish the ritual," said Snowdrop, interrupting.

"Ah, yes, about that part. The ritual. I have quite a lot of questions about it. So, to conclude, I'm connected to Docan, Regina sees it, but she doesn't know what it is. Then she dies and then *probably* learns about my true connection," said Tibi. He turned to Mia. "My God, I always believed dying meant just, you know, turning off the light."

"I told you there's something more," said Mia. "But we are all equal in the eyes of God."

"Now that's an amusing slogan," said Tibi, snorting.

"What? My mother's friend, the priest, used to say that. And he is right."

"Right. Anyway… she learns about my connection and starts appearing to me. I am driven, maybe by her struggle and appearances, to go to the gypsy campsite and undertake the ritual. By the way, why didn't you move your camp for so many years?"

"The Baba, the new Baba I mean, told us not to move. She said it will be bad luck if we move."

"But the Bulibasa is the one calling the shots," said Mia. "Was he happy to stay there?"

"No Bulibasa dares to go against what a Baba says," said Snowdrop, with a hint of pride in her voice.

"I see," said Mia. Then she turned to Tibi. "Okay, go on."

"Right. So, I reach the campsite, and then I do the ritual. What happened? What does the ritual mean?"

"Oh, that's a bond. It linked you with Docan and Regina."

"Yes, you said that already. But *what* is it?"

"It's a blood link."

"Jesus," said Tibi, "this is getting us nowhere."

"No," said Mia, touching his leg, "you're just asking the wrong questions." She looked at Snowdrop. "What he means is, what are its attributes? What is the link's purpose? What does it do?"

"Oh. It forces you to complete it."

"Okay. What does he have to complete? Does he need to find out who killed Docan?"

"Yes. And find his body. Then, if Docan is satisfied, the link will dissolve by itself."

"Yeah, like you said before. You also mentioned something about 'before the blood boy is born'."

"Yes. You either solve it, by finding the body and the killer, bringing peace to Docan and Regina, or you destroy the blood boy while he is still in the grave."

* * *

"We should go back," said the older policeman. He downed the remnants of his second beer and burped loudly. "You liked the burger, didn't you?" he asked Mike.

"Yeah, it wasn't bad," said Mike plainly. "But don't you want another one?"

"What, burger?"

"No, no. Beer."

"Oh," said the young one, "but we might have to—"

"Shush," said the older man. "Always ruining it. Yeah, let's have another one. Pay this check that Tony brought and let's get another round."

* * *

"I get it," said Tibi. "I know where the body is, and I know who did it. We just have to discover the body and that's that."

"Great," said Snowdrop. "Then it will all end."

"Yeah. I hope so. The dreams I'm having are horrible."

"Oh, yes. You must listen to the dreams, Baba used to say. They are talking to you through them."

"Yeah, I guess so. But they are always the same. Nothing changes," said Mia. "Right?" she added, turning toward Tibi.

"Yeah."

"Well, that means you are not listening."

"I see. Okay. The problem is they're not that direct. They seem to speak in riddles."

Snowdrop said nothing.

"Should we go?" asked Mia.

"Yes," said Snowdrop. "I want to go to my children."

"One more question, please," said Tibi. "I wanted to talk about the ritual. And the boy. I think… I think I saw it."

"The blood boy? This is good. It means the ritual worked."

"Yeah, *good* is a relative term," said Tibi. "But is it possible?"

"Of course it is," said Snowdrop. "That's the idea. The ritual says we put it to the ground—"

"And then it rises right back, yes," said Tibi.

"Right. We must do this ritual on a Tuesday. And the third day, on Thursday, he wakes up and gets out of the grave. But Baba always said it's best to do it right after Easter. That's the best moment, and it will most likely work."

"This is crazy," said Mia. "Have you ever seen such a thing rising?"

"Oh, no. That's how you can prevent the ritual from working. You desecrate the grave, or you stay around it so he cannot get out. That's the main reason we moved, I think," said Snowdrop. "Baba said we should go."

"But now, since he's out, there's nothing I can do," said Tibi, sighing.

"No. The ritual worked. He's out there."

"He. Why do you keep calling it 'he'?"

Snowdrop paused for a while. "I don't know," she said eventually. "That's how we always talked about him."

"Okay, fine," said Tibi. "I had the impression it… *he* helped me last time. Is that true?"

"Oh, yes. He always takes care of the linked people. Until you finish the ritual."

"And then what happens to him? He won't follow me to the city, right?"

"Oh, no. He just stays around the area he was born. He doesn't go too far. No."

"How far can he go?"

"I don't know. Around it. Far enough, I guess."

"Okay. And what happens when I finish the ritual?"

"He just disappears. Baba knows better, but I think they turn into a mound of dirt, and sometimes into red stones. I think it's red stones if the linked person dies before finishing the task. Or the other way around. I can't remember now," said Snowdrop, shaking her head. "Look, it's very hot in here. Can we go out? I think I answered all your questions."

"Yes, yes," said Mia, pushing Tibi out of the car. "Thank you very much for your help. Can we buy some flowers from you?"

"Oh, don't you worry," said Snowdrop, taking a deep breath once out of the car. "You don't have to do that."

"Oh, but I want to. Here," said Mia, handing her a few notes. "Thank you again for your help. And I'm so sorry about how those policemen—"

"Don't you worry. I'm used to it." She turned to her children, spoke to them quickly in her own language, and then they all walked away.

"Oh, sorry," said Tibi, taking a few quick steps to follow her. "One final question. What happened to the little girl?"

"Which girl?" asked Snowdrop, stopping and turning around. Her black hair waved as she did so, and her dark eyes sparkled under the burning sun.

"The one who, you know," said Tibi, trying to find his words. "The one covered in mud and on whom Baba—"

"Ah, yes."

"That girl," he said, sounding relieved. "She is okay, right?"

"Of course she is," said Snowdrop. "It is a great honor to be the one who gives the spark of life to the blood boy. Taking part in the ritual opens her up, and she might become a Baba someday, when she grows old." She stopped for a few seconds, her black eyes moving between Tibi and Mia. "Goodbye," she said, before departing.

* * *

"Oops," said the old policeman to the young one, looking out the window. "Mister policeman, look, your detainee is getting away. What are you going to do?"

"To hell with her," said the young policeman, taking another sip of his beer. "She wasn't arrested anyway."

"He, he, he," said the old one, wrapping his hands around the back of his neck, supporting his head. "You're starting to learn."

"Okay, then," said Mike, rising and throwing some money on the table. "For these last beers. Thank you for your help."

"What, leaving so early?" asked the older policeman, grinning.

"Yes. I'm not thirsty anymore," said Mike, and he hurried out of the tavern.

12 BLOOD BOY

"**S**he actually said the clay puppet is real?" asked Mike. He was sitting in the front passenger seat of Tibi's car, moving his gaze between Tibi, who was driving, and Mia in the backseat.

"Yeah," said Mia. "And the proper name is 'blood boy'. I mean, I don't think she's ever seen one. But I guess the community believes it's a real thing."

"Unbelievable," said Mike, shaking his head as he turned to face forward. "Next thing you're going to tell me is that Strigoi and Moroi are real."

"Those are creatures from the folklore around here, yes. But considering everything that has happened to me in the last few years, I think they could be real," said Tibi. "My grandmother told me quite a lot of stories about them. I never thought I'd be saying this, but I just hope I never meet one. I can't imagine a world in which such creatures were around, you know, day by day. I would be the first to die, I can tell you that. At least, according to my grandma, they tend to stay in the mountain forests—a place where I rarely go."

"But did your grandma ever tell you anything about the blood boy? Until today I never thought something like this could be real."

"No. Wait. What? You thought I made up the story about the blood boy?" asked Tibi, as he drove along the beautiful switchback road surrounded by tall pine trees.

"No. I mean, I thought *you* believed it was real."

"Pfft," said Tibi with a wistful smile. "Did you think *I* killed Horza?"

"No! I mean… it did cross my mind," said Mike. "Who wouldn't have considered it? You see things that aren't there, you are attacked in the woods, and then *something* strange kills the attacker. It could have been your subconscious, trying to protect you."

"Don't tell me you're a psychoanalyst now," said Tibi.

"No. It's just, I've seen some movies. You do a very bad thing and somehow your brain tells you something else happened."

"Yeah, I know what you mean. Good thing I'm in the clear now," said Tibi, his smile evaporating.

"Yeah. I only have one question. Two questions, actually. First, why don't you call it in?"

"Call what in? The attack?"

"Yeah. Now we know you're innocent, you should call it in."

"Ah, but I already knew I was innocent when I decided in the first place *not* to call it in," said Tibi, laughing. "And the decision still stands. First I must find that thing hidden in the pile of construction materials. And then, with that information to hand, I can call it in."

"And hopefully that will be the end of it," said Mia, leaning forward to pat Tibi's right shoulder.

"Should we buy you a shovel?" asked Mike.

"Why?"

"So Emi doesn't know you're going into the woods to dig. You know, entering the woods after Horza disappeared, with a shovel… Get it?"

"Yeah, I get it. But we'll have to take the same model, so it's the same as in my dream. And I don't think we have much time to waste."

"Okay. And what do you think you'll find in that pile?" asked Mike.

"You know, after talking to Snowdrop, I've been thinking."

"Wait, her name is Snowdrop?" asked Mike, laughing.

"Yeah."

"It's a beautiful name. Stop it," said Mia.

"What's with these names?" He then started talking, trying to fake a gypsy accent. "Look, honey, we'll have a new child soon. For the best results, we should use 'Snowdrop', 'Anvil' or 'Disrupt', whatever fits best."

"You're an idiot," said Tibi, chuckling as Mia huffed. "So, now, back to it. What were you asking?"

"I asked what you think you'll find in that pile," said Mike.

"Right. So, after talking to Snowdrop, I don't think it will be Docan. Not at first. He is down there, for sure, but I think he's buried deep. Horza couldn't have been stupid enough to leave him too close to the surface. The corpse might have attracted bears or wolves. No, I think I'll find something incriminating, like his toolbox or something."

"Ah, the one that Ana said he carried around?" asked Mia.

"Yeah. What else could I find that would link back to a nomadic gypsy? They have no ID, so his wallet wouldn't help. Maybe I'll find his clothes, covered in blood. Or the murder weapon, with Docan's blood and Horza's fingerprints on it. But in that case, how could we know that it's Docan's blood? So we'll need something else, something incriminating. But I don't think Horza will have made such a mistake."

"Okay," said Mike. "Why is this relevant then? Why would the dream point you there?"

"Because I can then use what I find to convince the police to dig into the pile, to uncover his body," said Tibi, winking at him.

"I see," said Mike, nodding. "Smart. Okay. I can see that happening."

"The only concern…" said Mia, then stopped.

"What?" asked Tibi. "What is it?"

"Nothing, it's just… have you noticed the back of the guesthouse?"

"Which guesthouse?"

"Horza's, dufus!"

"Ah, that," said Tibi, laughing. "Now that I think of it, not really. I just saw the back fence and that gate which we opened to go into the forest."

"Well, there are houses nearby, several of which have a direct view over the yard. Someone could have seen him carrying a body."

"Hmm, I see," said Tibi. "Then he probably moved it at night.

Or properly wrapped in something."

"Yeah, or in pieces," said Mike.

"Yuck!" said Mia, grimacing.

Everyone paused for a few minutes, lost in thought.

"Right. And what was the second question?" asked Mia, breaking the silence.

"Yeah, that. So, my second question is…" said Mike, talking slowly.

"Ah, I know," said Tibi, laughing. "Here we go. What is it now? You mention my height? Being a vegetarian? Going to call me gay for eating strawberries? What?"

"No, no," said Mike, faking an innocent tone, but clearly holding back a smile. "I was just wondering, is it true you're a gypsy?"

The three of them burst into laughter.

"Yeah. I said my father was like me: a bit darker than the rest. But now that I think of it, my grandfather on my mother's side was two shades darker. I always thought he was like that because he worked the field. You know, being a farmer, he could have been tanned all the time. I didn't meet my great-grandparents, so I don't know what happened there."

"You could ask your parents," said Mia. "Your mother has black hair, doesn't she? Just like Snowdrop."

"I guess so. I mean, her skin is lighter than mine, but, true, she has black hair and eyes. Hmm… Snowdrop could be onto something."

"My God, so many jokes roll into my head right now," said Mike, laughing.

"Yeah, I know," said Tibi, grinning. "I'll find out something about you, at some point, and then I'll have my revenge."

"Yeah, I'm fat, so that's easy. Otherwise, nothing exotic about me."

They all smiled as the car made yet another curve along the national road.

"I wonder how your children will look," said Mike suddenly, pursing his lips in a self-satisfied smirk. "I mean, you," he said, turning back to look at Mia, "are blond, with blue eyes and milk-white skin. While you, Tibi, are—how should I put it?—plain ugly."

"Ha, ha," said Tibi. "Thank you for that rambling diatribe and—

"

"Hey, guys," said Mia, interrupting their exchange. "When you stop horsing around, let's talk about what to do next."

"Yeah, that's a good idea," said Tibi. "Sorry, I relaxed a bit, now that I know I'm not crazy."

"I know. But we need to finish this, so we can all go home."

"Yup, you're right. So, I plan on going back to the waste pile. I'll dig into it, find the object, and call it in. That's basically it."

"I guess it depends on what you find," said Mike.

"Yeah, of course. But I suspect it's either the toolbox or some sort of metal coffin."

"Why metal?" asked Mia.

"In my dream, my spade struck something metal each time before I woke up."

* * *

They pulled up in front of Horza's guesthouse at around four. They were greeted by Emi, who seemed concerned.

"Hello," he said, bowing briefly. "Welcome back."

"Hi, Emi," said Mia, with a tired smile. "How are you?"

"I'm fine. In fact, not that fine."

"What's happened?" said Mia, stopping on the stairs and looking at him, as the others pressed on to open the main door.

"I can't find Mr. Horza. I mean, his car is right here. He must have come to the guesthouse last night. But I can't find him anywhere. And his phone seems to be dead."

"Um," said Tibi, turning around, "maybe he went for a hike?"

"Where, in the forest?" asked Emi, looking straight at Tibi. "Have you seen him? You were in the forest last night."

"No, no," said Tibi, waving his hands. "I just found that pile of construction materials. And then I came back. It was too creepy."

"I see," said Emi. "I'm thinking of calling the police."

"Yeah, maybe you should do that," said Tibi. "We have to go now. Oh, by the way," he said, turning once more toward Emi. "I need that shovel again. May I borrow it?"

"Yes. By the way, I found it lying next to the shed. In the future, please don't leave it outside. We have thieves around here. Just take it to your room. Or you can leave it somewhere in the lobby. Anyway, somewhere where people can't take it easily."

"Yeah, got it," said Tibi. "Sorry, I didn't know."

"No worries," said Emi. "I'll bring it here."

"Thank you. I have to change my clothes, then I'll come pick it up."

* * *

"I'll go now," said Tibi, coming out of the bathroom and pulling on a fresh T-shirt.

"What? Alone?" asked Mia. "No way. We're coming with you."

"No chance," said Tibi.

"What? Why? Where are you going?"

"I am going to the pile. I'll dig for that thing. Then I'll call the police."

"We're coming to help."

"Just like last time, I don't want you to risk your lives. We have that blood boy following us. Do you want to be around if it decides you're an enemy the first time you disagree with me?"

"No. But do you want to be alone, with a blood boy roaming around?"

"Not really. But you heard Snowdrop. He's going to keep me safe. So, all things considered, I might be the safest person in the woods. But I must go alone. I don't want to worry about you. Ah, damn," he said, stopping in his tracks.

"What?"

"I just realized, Emi is looking for Horza, and I'm going into the woods with a shovel. All alone."

"Ah… I hope he doesn't think you're going to bury him."

"Jesus," said Tibi, stopping to think. "Ah, but I would have done it yesterday, right? I mean, if I'd been the one to kill him, I would have buried him yesterday."

"I guess," said Mia, frowning as Tibi left the room.

* * *

Tibi found the shovel leaning next to the counter, where Emi

160

was sitting. At Tibi's approach, Emi lifted his gaze from the computer screen.

"Oh, hello Mr. Coman. All good?"

"Yeah. I'm going out for a few hours. I'll be back later this evening."

"Oh, but a storm is coming," said Emi, glancing through the window. "See those dark clouds? They're massing. It will get dark soon, even if it's not that late."

"I know," said Tibi, pausing as he tried to come up with a plausible explanation. "There's something I have to do though, and tomorrow I must return to the city. I don't know when I'll have time to come back here again."

"No worries. Do as you wish," said Emi, trying a smile.

"See you," said Tibi, heading out. *That went well,* thought Tibi. *Yeah, 'something I have to do', not creepy at all. Oh well.* He went around the building to the back.

He looked around, for the first time really, at the surroundings. The Three Bears guesthouse stood behind him, and straight ahead, behind a fence with an open gate, was the forest. Left and right of Horza's property were other houses and guesthouses, and plenty of windows faced the backyard.

Difficult to carry a body into the forest in plain daylight and not be seen. And at night that damn light shines into the corridor, making me see shapes of tall ghosts. That lamppost ruins everything. Mia was right. So, I guess they did it at night, hoping people were asleep or, as Mike said, they just carried pieces.

He squeezed the shovel, passed through the back gate and entered the forest.

* * *

As he walked, leaves struck his face and storm clouds gathered above.

He could sense something was watching him, yet he felt safe.

"Hey, blood boy," said Tibi, suddenly, his voice sounding strange in the forest. "It's good that you're keep me safe. But don't kill anyone, you hear?"

He continued his advance, finally seeing the pile.

He took a few more steps, then stopped, looking around as he suddenly realized something.

Where the hell is Horza? He was supposed to be here. What if he's alive? Or maybe wild animals got him.

He looked around. *And where is his pistol?* He turned left and right, squatting and touching the grass.

Still, he couldn't find any clues, so he turned to face the pile once more.

He started climbing it with nimble steps. He reached the part in the back, the one in his dreams, and he heaved away the few remaining metal sheets and bars.

He now had full access to the dusty, white materials.

Using the shovel, he started to push away the rubble, as the first rumble of thunder echoed through the mountain valley. After a few minutes, the shovel hit something hard. In the same moment, the first drop of rain landed on his back.

"This is it," he said, happiness engulfing him.

He squatted, throwing away the shovel, and pushing away further pieces of drywall with his hands. Below it, a metal toolbox was now visible.

"So that's what it was," he said, shaking his head. "Mr. Horza, you weren't that smart, were you?"

He moved a few steps away, grabbed the shovel, and started to clear out the debris around the metal box.

The first few drops of rain soon turned into a heavy summer downpour which soaked him to the skin. But the shovel did a good job of freeing the toolbox, and soon enough Tibi was squatting, shovel by his side, grabbing the handles on the side of the box.

He pulled, yet the box didn't move.

"Come on," he said, spitting as some water ran down his face, into his mouth. "I'm wet like a frog."

He pulled once more, his body moving up, then falling back onto the toolbox as he grew tired.

Suddenly, he felt a vibration.

* * *

"Ah, there it is," said Mia as she moved a pillow away, uncovering her phone. "Found it," she yelled toward the door.

"Let's go."

"We're going to the same restaurant, right?" asked Mike, salivating. "I'm starving."

"Yeah, me too. Let's go."

"So, Tibi didn't want us around," said Mike, heading down the stairs.

"No."

"I say, after we eat, we go find him."

"No," said Mia. "I mean, it's dangerous. I guess he's right not to want us there."

"But I want to help him!"

"Yes, so do I. But there's nothing we can do for now." Mia sighed. "I sat by the phone, hoping he'd call if he needed anything. So far, nothing. Oh, and make sure you take an umbrella or something. It's pouring out there."

"Yeah. By the way, why don't *you* call *him*?"

* * *

Tibi looked down at his pocket, where his phone was.

"Jesus!" he said out loud, digging out the phone. "Yes? What's up?" He was yelling, trying to speak over the noise made by the rain.

"How are you, babe?"

"I'm fine. I reached the pile, and I think I've found the object."

"What is it?"

"It looks like the toolbox. I haven't been able to get ahold of it yet. I'm still trying to take it out. But soon, I'll know."

"Why do you want to take it out? Why not call the police to look at it?"

"Having dreamt about it for so many years, I just have to pull it out. They told me to find it, so I want to take the toolbox out and hold it in my hands. I think I have to."

"But don't open it! You might destroy any evidence."

"Yeah, you're right. I'll just pull it out and then call the police."

"So, I take it you're safe?"

"I'm soaked, but I guess so. Yet, Horza is gone."

"What do you mean?"

"It's not here. The body's not here."

163

"Do you think he survived?"

"Maybe. Or maybe it was animals. Look, I have to go. It's raining like hell over here," he said, putting down the phone. "Good thing this phone is water resistant," he added to himself, grabbing the toolbox once more.

He started pulling, groaning loud.

"Come on!" he yelled, as he fell back onto the box again. "What the hell?"

Suddenly, the ground collapsed, and Tibi fell deep into the pile, screaming.

* * *

"That was a spectacular steak!" said Mike, sipping from his glass of wine.

"It sure looked like it," said Mia.

"Your mushroom stew with polenta looked great as well."

"Yeah, I loved it," said Mia, picking up her glass of wine.

"So, do we call him again?"

"Yeah, why not."

* * *

Tibi woke up. He could hear water drops, and he immediately realized parts of his body were very wet. He opened his eyes and moved his head slightly. He was lying in a pool of water.

"Eww," he said, pushing himself up. *The clothes are probably ruined forever.*

He quickly looked around. He was inside a cavern of some sort, but he could barely make out his surroundings.

"What the hell?" he said, looking up. *Why is it so dark?*

He saw no opening.

Jesus. How far did I fall? He looked up at the ceiling, yet he couldn't see anything. *Better yet, where did I fall from?*

He took out his phone and turned on the flashlight. He moved it around. He soon saw the shovel next to him and he reached for it.

"Ah!" he said with disgust, realizing he was standing in a pool of blood. It was wide, more than a dozen feet, and it seemed to cover the entire cavern. The blood was a few inches deep and small ripples formed at his every move.

He grabbed the shovel and then looked around the cavern.

It was a relatively square cave about two dozen feet by two dozen feet, with rounded edges. And it was all dug into the ground. It was like an upside-down square clay bowl.

The walls were made of brown clay and he could see some spots scattered around the cave's mud walls. He took a few steps closer and saw that the spots were, in fact, black rocks.

Suddenly, on the wall he was investigating, he saw some of the dirt 'popping', and a slow stream of liquid started oozing out, trickling down the wall. He aimed the flashlight there.

"Blood," he said, taking a step back.

He realized the entire wall was covered in slow-dripping blood, which eventually ran into the pool in the middle.

"What the hell is this?" he said, his voice trembling. He turned around, fast, looking at the walls and the ceiling, trying to find a way out.

The ceiling was about fifteen feet up, yet, just like first time he'd checked, he could see no opening. He *could* see a darker part of a wall, pitch black, the size of an opened umbrella. He went there and discovered it was a tunnel. He squatted, looking inside. It looked like it went up.

"Could this be the exit?" he mumbled, trying to see deeper inside. His flashlight was not strong enough to see far, yet the muddy tunnel was clearly rising at an angle. "Maybe there's a better way out," he mumbled, standing and looking around.

He noticed the wall opposite looked a bit different and took a few steps closer, splashing through the wide blood pool, pointing the flashlight at the wall.

"Bones!" he said, stopping his advance. Some were sticking out of the wall, white against the dark clay. "Docan?" said Tibi, as a shiver ran down his spine.

He had an idea. He pressed a few buttons on the phone and took a few flashlight photos.

It was then he spotted an opening at the edge of the wall with the bones, no wider than four feet. It was right at the base, and a small stream of blood was passing under the wall, coming from the pond behind him.

"Maybe this is the exit," he said, squatting and pushing the flashlight inside. "I guess not, as it's going downwards."

Suddenly, he felt there was something in there, waiting for him. He froze as he heard a faint humming coming from within the opening. He turned off his flashlight and waited for his eyes to adjust. In the meantime, he kept listening.

Once his vision improved, he thought he glimpsed a warm, moving light. He gripped his shovel tight as he leaned closer.

Should I go in? But it's not an exit. It's going down. Damn it! Something is there. I think I must.

Tibi sighed as he ducked, trying to fit inside. He crawled forward, his head often hitting the clay ceiling above, making him turn his flashlight back on. It allowed him to see a few steps in front, but the rest of the tunnel was pitch black. The floor was soaking wet with the blood trickling downwards.

I'm an idiot, he thought, as he took a few more steps, going deeper.

Suddenly, he slipped and tumbled forward.

When he opened his eyes, he saw a warm light dancing on the clay wall next to him. He turned his head and pushed himself up a few inches, looking around.

He was in another cave, just like the last one: some sort of upside-down bowl about two dozen feet wide. Only this one was round and the ceiling was lower. In the middle was a wooden fire, spreading light all around.

Across the fire, by the rounded wall, he could see two shadows. It seemed to be two people sitting cross-legged on the floor, two arm-lengths between them.

"Oh, hello," said Tibi, rising while looking around him. The shovel was to his right, about three feet away, while the phone was a few steps to his left.

"Hello," came a cawing woman's voice from the shadow to the right.

Tibi stood careful not to hit the ceiling. He took a few tiny steps.

"I know you," he said eventually. "I've heard your voice bef— Ah, it's you! Regina!"

166

Regina finally became visible as a dancing flame moved within the fire, casting a trembling light over her face. She was large, dressed in the same colorful dress Tibi remembered. She said nothing, looking straight at him.

"So, I guess this is Docan," said Tibi, looking at the person to the left. He could see the black clothes, skinny hands and body, yet Docan was so tall that his head remained in the shadows.

Docan, just like Regina, remained silent.

"What… Why am I here?" said Tibi, taking another step toward them.

At the same time, Docan and Regina raised their right hands, urging Tibi to stop.

He took a quick step back, looking at the ground. It was dark brown dirt, yet little pools of blood were all around. The entire cave seemed moist.

Tibi sat, trying to avoid a blood pool, and looked at Docan and Regina.

"So," he said eventually, "why are we here?"

"You tell us," said Docan. "You came to us."

"Yes, well, I was looking for the thing. You know, the one you told me so many times to find. I found the toolbox and when I pulled—"

Suddenly, he saw something to his left, out of the corner of his eye. He turned his head. The fire pushed some light to that side and he could see an opening scooped into the side of the cave.

Inside it was Horza. He was sitting down, like in a dirt armchair, and he seemed to have passed out. There was dried blood on his chin, mouth and chest. He was wheezing, and he didn't look good at all.

"He's alive!" yelled Tibi.

Regina and Docan kept silent.

"Now it makes sense. I came for him," said Tibi, turning toward Regina and Docan.

"You came for nothing," said Docan.

"I can't leave him here to die."

Regina stared at him for a second, then cocked her head. "He tried to kill you."

"True. But I can't just stand by and let someone die, not in good

167

conscience."

No one said anything.

"Can I take him?"

"No," said Docan.

"Please."

No answer.

Tibi leaned to his left, trying to get up.

"Stop," said Regina, just as a new shadow appeared behind Tibi, emerging from the wall, somewhere near Horza.

It was the blood boy, who took a few small steps, moving between Tibi and Horza.

The blood boy was just like a clay sock puppet. It was red and seemed void of any bones or joints, its limbs bending like pool noodles.

Tibi let out a yell, rising fast and taking two quick steps back. The blood boy had no face, no eyes, yet he felt it was looking straight at him. "So it's true. I guess deep down I hoped this… thing didn't exist."

Silence.

"Please," said Tibi, getting ahold of himself and sitting back down, facing the fire. "I can't leave him here."

"You cannot take him," said Docan.

"You must go out and find it," said Regina.

"If you don't find it, you cannot solve it."

"Yes, I get it. I will go out and find it. I know where it is. But I want to take Horza with me."

"You cannot take him."

Tibi kept silent, thinking. "What must I do to be allowed to take him out?"

No one answered.

"I can't solve this for you if I can't take him out."

"Lies!" yelled Regina, and blood boy took a quick step closer to Tibi, staying between him and Horza.

Tibi raised his left hand defensively. "Wait! It's not a lie. Soon the police will come. If Horza remains missing they will suspect I killed him. He will—"

"We don't care," said Docan. "He deserves to die. And you, you have to find it."

"You didn't find it," chimed in Regina.

"No, no, I didn't," said Tibi, leaning over to grab his phone. He had a full-strength signal, even though he was underground.

Should I call Mia to hear this?

Eventually, he turned on the camera and pressed Record.

* * *

"It's going straight to voicemail," said Mia.

"Try again."

"I tried five times!" she yelled, slamming the phone onto the table. "Sorry."

"No worries."

"Do you think… Do you think he's—"

"No! Stop it. Don't go there. There's probably no reception in that forest. We're deep in the mountains, you know. The signal doesn't cover every meadow and cliff."

"Yeah, I hope that's the reason."

* * *

"Look," said Tibi, "we're wasting time. And Horza is dying."

"This is good," said Docan.

"It probably is," said Tibi, "but I cannot leave him here. So, unless you plan to kill me and lose all hope of solving your problem, let me take him out with me."

Tibi rose, taking the few remaining steps toward Horza.

Suddenly, Docan and Regina started screaming. It was deafening, and Tibi flinched, twisting to the right to look at the two of them. They were still sitting down, hands by the side of their bodies. He could see Regina's mouth open, and flecks of spit were coming out through her dark, decayed teeth.

Tibi turned around. He went for the shovel, while Regina and Docan continued screaming. He then took the last step and reached for Horza.

Blood boy came between them and pushed him back.

Tibi used his free hand, pushing blood boy to the left. As he touched the puppet's clay body he felt the cold texture of wet soil.

Much to his surprise, his hand sank into the blood boy's body. The red dirt moved around his fingers like kinetic sand, and a second later Tibi's hand emerged on the other side. The blood boy hadn't moved.

"Shit!" said Tibi, as blood boy pushed him again, vigorously, making him take a step back.

He swung his right arm and the shovel cut blood boy in half. As the top part fell, the whole body sank to the ground like goo. Tibi froze, watching at the red clay molded back into the shape of the boy.

"God damn it!" he yelled, yet his cry was muffled by the loud screams still coming from Docan and Regina.

Tibi took a step forward, hitting blood boy with his right boot. Yet, just like before, his foot moved through its body, passing out on the other side.

Still, a small part of the red clay splattered onto the dirt wall behind Horza. And as it struck it turned into blood and started trickling down.

"Aha," said Tibi. He aimed his shovel and hit the boy again, this time with the wide side of the spade. It struck true, and even though parts of the clay moved around the obstruction, a lot of it was thrown onto the wall, thickening the blood stream.

The remaining clay forming blood boy's body tumbled down, and Tibi dropped the shovel, grabbed Horza's right hand and a fistful of his shirt and started pulling him toward the tunnel leading to the tall room.

He took a few steps, then he realized he'd left the shovel.

Eh, who needs that, he thought, as he took another step.

Looking back, he could see that blood boy was reforming. He was standing in a small pool of blood, which he seemed to be sucking into the clay that was forming him. And, little by little, the body was rejuvenating. It would soon be the same size as before.

"Shit," said Tibi, again not loud enough to be heard over Docan and Regina's screams. He realized they never stopped screaming, not even to take a breath.

He still couldn't see Docan's face. Tibi dropped Horza and dashed toward his shovel. He grabbed it, laid it on top of Horza's body, and then resumed his retreat, pulling Horza by his wrists.

He had just reached the tunnel going up when blood boy finished reforming.

"Oh, shut the hell up!" he yelled, looking at the two people across the fire. "I'll help you, so let me be!"

Still, they continued to yell, while Tibi lowered his body and took the first step into the tunnel, pulling Horza after him. Horza seemed to be unconscious, and his head lolled with every move.

Blood boy rushed forward and reached Horza's leg. He started advancing up his body, over his waist and soon up to his neck.

"Go away!" Tibi dropped Horza and pushed blood boy back with his shovel.

Still, he couldn't swing like before; he now risked hitting Horza. Blood boy came back.

"Damn it," said Tibi. He grabbed Horza and pulled him one step, then pushed blood boy to the side with the shovel. He could barely move through the narrow place, but his swing made blood boy decrease in size once more. "If you kill me, you die too!" Tibi yelled at the relentless clay puppet. "And the ritual will not be completed," he shouted down the tunnel, "and you two screaming idiots will never get your peace!"

He pulled again, then dropped the man, grabbed the shovel and pushed blood boy once more.

He did this about twelve times and soon realized the screaming was now faint. Two more steps and he was out of the tunnel, back in the square room.

He set Horza down next to the large pool of blood. He checked his phone and saw it was still recording.

"You cannot take him," came Regina's voice from behind him.

"No, you cannot," added Docan.

Tibi turned quickly, his heart freezing. He stopped the recording and turned on the flashlight.

Docan's face remained covered in darkness, no matter how much he tried to move the flashlight in that direction, yet Regina was visible. They were both standing in front of the other tunnel. the one which, it was now clear to him, led outside.

* * *

171

"I think we should call the police," said Mike, looking worried.

"Are you sure?" said Mia.

"Yeah. I mean, his cell is dead. God knows what's happened to him."

"Okay, fine," said Mia, sighing. "You call the police. I'll keep on trying to reach him."

* * *

"Let me pass!" yelled Tibi, enraged. "What the hell is wrong with you? I have to save this man!"

"You can go. But leave him here," said Docan, in the same calm-but-firm voice.

"He is guilty."

"Yes, okay, fine, he is. But we should let the law take its course." Docan and Regina said nothing.

"I will take him out."

"You will not," said Docan and Regina at the same time.

"You know what?" said Tibi after a few moments. "I've had it with you. You want me to help, then let me have this."

"No," the choir answered.

Tibi stopped. He looked around. He squatted and grabbed the shovel, taking a step toward Docan and Regina.

"You really want to do that?" asked Regina, her eyes unflinching, as blood boy took a step to the side, getting between Tibi and his target.

Suddenly, blood boy changed his shape into a long, thin stream of clay. It was just like water bursting out of a hose, yet this was red dirt. He sprang forward and slammed into Tibi's face.

Tibi closed his mouth just in time, although the move was so unexpected that bits of the red clay managed to get in, attacking his senses. The smell and taste of blood was intoxicating, and he fell on the ground, dizzy.

Yet the attacker immediately departed. Tibi spat out the remaining blood and quickly grabbed his phone, which he'd dropped when falling.

"You bastard," said Tibi, taking a step forward and swinging the shovel.

A large part of blood boy was thrown onto the wall, and Tibi swung again, toward the other side, sending another section flying.

The swings kept on falling. Still, blood boy seemed not to care. He was standing in the middle of the large pool of blood, growing back faster than Tibi could reduce him.

"I come from blood," said Regina, as Tibi's rage ended.

"I come from blood," said Docan.

"He comes from blood," said Regina, looking toward blood boy.

"And you come from blood," said Docan, pointing.

"Enough with this blood shit already! You know what? We might all come from blood. And, as Mia said, we are all equal in the eyes of God. But all this," he said, waving his hands around, "I've had my fair share of religion classes in school. I know it's not Christian. What's with all this blood? This is not from God. It looks more like hell, really."

He turned around and, using the shovel, cut a long vertical line into the wall behind him, to the left of the white bones. Larger drops of blood came out, tricking down.

"No!" said Docan and Regina at the same time, as Tibi shifted the spade to draw a second, horizontal line.

"Oh yes. Let's see how this looks inside this hell hole," said Tibi, finishing off a cross on the wall.

Docan and Regina let out a painful scream.

"Oh, I'll do some more then," said Tibi, moving to the right of the bones, where Horza still lay, passed out.

"Stop!" yelled Regina, as he finished a second cross.

Tibi could see the ground around the cuts turning to stone, just like the stones already scattered in the wall. And, soon enough, their color turned from red to black and blood stopped tricking from them.

"I can go on forever," said Tibi. "I'll fill this damn room with a million crosses if I have to! But, by God, I will take Horza with me."

Regina and Docan watched him in silence, and Tibi took a step toward the wall to his left.

"Wait!" said Regina, suddenly. "You can go."

She and Docan moved to the side, leaving the tunnel open.

"If you hurt me," said Tibi, "you know I won't be able to complete my part of the ritual. And you'll be stuck in this world

173

forever."

Regina and Docan said nothing, and Tibi pulled Horza out. He kept his shovel close, in case of further attack. But Regina, Docan and blood boy just stared at him as he pulled Horza through the blood pond and then into the tunnel going up.

He tugged and tugged, groaning and puffing, and a few dozen pulls later he reached the surface, emerging next to a mound of dirt near the pile of construction materials. Tibi leaned Horza against the mound and sat next to him, positioning himself between the hole in the ground and Horza. Tibi reached for his phone.

* * *

"Where the hell have you been?" said Mia, almost yelling. "I've been calling you for two hours!"

"Two hours? Impossible. And I was right here. A bit underground, in a tunnel of some sort. I'll tell you all about it. But I've found Horza. He's alive!"

"Really?"

"Yeah. But I've got to hang up, to call for an ambulance. Why did you call me?"

"I wanted to know what happened to you, that's why," said Mia, puffing. "Oh, and we already called the police."

"Why?"

"We were afraid something had bad happened to you!"

"Okay, okay. Don't yell," said Tibi, sighing through the phone. "I'm fine. It's good you called the police. When I call for an ambulance, I'll tell them who I am. By the way, I think I've also found Docan's body. Bones, actually."

"Wow! Really? That too? Good. Tell me all about it!"

"I can't. I'm too tired. It was horrible. I'm happy it's raining. It washes off all the blood."

"What blood?"

"Not mine. It's nothing. Oh!"

"What?"

"My God, where did all the blood go?"

"What blood? Tiberiu Coman, what is going on?"

"Nothing. I mean, I've been in a place with a lot of blood. I fell in it. And my clothes are muddy, yes, but I can't see any blood on them. Look, I have to call the ambulance, and I need my phone's flashlight to check my clothes."

"Okay, okay, I'll hang up. Stay safe."

She hung up, while Mike, who was sitting across the table, questioned her with his eyes.

"Yeah, I found him, finally. And he found them. Both Docan and Horza. He said he's been in a tunnel."

"What? For two hours? And what were you saying about blood?"

Mia said nothing, shrugging.

* * *

Tiberiu turned on the flashlight and checked his clothes. He was dirty and muddy, and the pouring rain was making the brown mud run down his body. Still, there was no sign of blood anywhere.

He turned to the shovel. It was clean as well.

What the hell? Where have I been? Didn't I use this damn shovel to hit that blood boy? Why isn't it bloody? Was it…was it all in my head? But I found Horza. He turned to look at the wheezing man next to him. *Could Mike be right? Is my mind hiding things from me?*

He turned off the flashlight and called the emergency number.

"Hello? Yes, I need an ambulance. I'm in the woods by Horza's guesthouse. Yes, the Three Bears, but follow the trail behind the guesthouse into the woods. I've found Horza, the owner. He's hurt. I don't know. He's wheezing and he's unconscious. Yes, please. I'll tell you where to find me."

No, it can't be, he thought, turning the flashlight on once more. *I saw all those things. I was definitely in a place, a strange place, that exists, yet it probably has its own rules. Yes, that must be it.*

He continued to ponder by Horza's side, until, forty minutes later, a policeman and three emergency care assistants came running up the hill.

"Over here!" yelled Tibi, waving.

"What happened here?" asked the policeman.

"I found him, deep in that hole," said Tibi, pointing to his right.

"What hole?" asked the policeman.

He looked at the policeman and, upon seeing his face, turned to the right.

There was no hole.

"I mean…" said Tibi, shaking his head. "Sorry. I'm tired and cold. You know, I found him over there and then I moved him here. I was a bit confused. Yes. I moved him onto this mound."

The three care assistants cut open Horza's shirt.

"Oh," said one of them, a woman in her forties.

Tibi turned. Horza's chest was badly bruised. It was dark red all over.

"Jesus," said Tibi. "It's a miracle he's alive."

"Who the hell did this?" said the policeman, his jaw dropping.

"I don't know," said Tibi. "It must be some animal, I think."

"Jesus. Okay. What's your name? Do you have some ID?"

* * *

Half an hour later, Tibi watched as two of the medical personnel carried Horza away on a stretcher, the third holding a flashlight, lighting their way through the trees. He stared after them long after they'd disappeared out of sight.

"This sounds far-fetched," said the policeman, dragging Tibi's attention back to the clearing.

"Trust me. Docan's body is in that pile over there," said Tibi, getting up. "Come on. The rain has stopped. This is a good moment."

They reached the back pile through which Tibi had fallen.

"Careful," said Tibi, "It's not completely stable."

But now it looked as it had before, with no hole visible. And in the middle, there was no toolbox, just construction waste.

"Are you sure you didn't hit your head or anything?"

"Yes," said Tibi, his throat constricted. "I'm telling you, the body is around here somewhere. And I bet it's under this pile."

"The body of a gypsy?"

"Of a human being."

"Yeah, well. We'll check it out and keep in touch," said the policeman, making a face and turning around.

"Yeah," said Tibi, trailing off. "You should check this. And, as I said, I have to go back to the city, but you have all my details."

"Yes, okay," said the policeman, walking away, seeming not to care.

Tibi waited for a few minutes, until he was alone again. He looked around, yet he still couldn't see the opening in the ground.

"Jesus," he mumbled, reaching for his phone once more.

He waited for a few dozen seconds, until someone finally answered.

"Oh, hello Ana. I hope it's not too late. Look, I really need your help. Could you talk to your brother-in-law, Julian? Yes, I have the number, but I need you to call him."

After he hung up, he leaned back and took a deep breath. He then called Mia and had a long chat about everything and nothing, like they used to do when they were dating.

"Oh, I think some more policemen have arrived," said Tibi into the phone, a few dozen minutes later. "I'll talk to them and then come home, okay?"

13 DIGGING

It was almost midnight, but the light was bright. A portable generator was running, powering two powerful LED searchlights.

"Keep digging," yelled a policeman, as about half a dozen more searched through the rubble.

"So, what do we have here?" asked another policeman, reaching Tibi.

"Hello."

"Oh, hi," said the policeman. "I'm Julian, Ana's brother-in-law. What's happened?" He was tall, broad-shouldered, and probably in his late thirties. He had a round face, and his nose was a bit crooked. Still, aside from the nose, he resembled his brother, Ana's husband, quite well.

"Hi Julian. Thank you for your help today. I'm lucky I met Ana. It was kind of her to call you."

"No problem. She's told me quite a lot of strange things."

"Yeah, about that," said Tibi, turning toward the pile. "I found something here, I mean, other than Horza, who was injured. And by putting other pieces of information together, a lot of which Ana helped with, I've come to realize that Docan's body must be somewhere in this pile."

"Yes, she said I should come dig for a body here. But who's Docan?"

"He's a gypsy, from the campsite. The nomads. He used to work the village as a handyman, for a meal and some money. And I think Horza killed him."

"Wow," said Julian, stopping his writing and looking at Tibi. "How can you know that?"

"Horza attacked me when I came out here to investigate. He said I should have minded my own business."

"He's in the hospital. Did you fight with him?"

"No, no. I ran away."

"When did this happen? Why didn't you call it in?"

"I needed to talk to the gypsies first. I was still piecing things together. And I wasn't hurt, so I thought there was no need to press charges. But now, now I can talk."

"I see," said Julian, pondering. "I mean… it's a bit strange. How did you escape?"

"Nothing special. I just ran."

"And what stopped Mr. Horza from running after you?"

"I don't know," said Tibi. "I mean, he tried to catch me, but at some point he lost me. It was a dark night."

"Ah, I see. Okay. So when was this?"

"Last night."

"And then we found him almost dead?"

"I found him."

"Yeah, exactly," said Julian. "*You* found him."

"What's wrong with that?"

"You tell me."

"This exchange sounds like dialogue from a B movie," said Tibi, scoffing.

"Well, I'm sure you can understand why I might think this is odd."

"Are you accusing me of anything, Officer Capata?"

"No. Not yet at least. Go ahead, tell me, is there any other information?"

"Information?"

"Other details. For example, how did you know where to come and look for the body? Ana was rather convincing over the phone, but how can *you* know it's here? I'm starting to believe I've been had. I should have waited to investigate, before bringing all these men from the national police. Why shouldn't I just tell them the lead has turned out to be false and give everyone back their evening?"

"Look, I've been through a lot," said Tibi. "But I'll tell you what I know. I found a toolbox in that waste pile. It was there. I couldn't check it properly as rain was pouring in. Then the ground collapsed, I think, and now the toolbox is buried deep. Anyway, I believe that toolbox will somehow link Horza to the killing. Which, mind you, happened four years ago."

"Killing him here? Who would come here to kill a gypsy? And especially a well-placed guy like Mr. Horza?"

"No, not here. He was killed in Horza's guesthouse, in Room 26. Surely Ana told you about the room. Then Horza disposed of the body here."

"I see."

"What?"

"We'll have to check all this. And I need to know how you learned about it."

"Could we continue this tomorrow?" said Tibi. "Look at me. I'm dead tired. I can barely stand."

"Okay, fine. Where will you be?"

"At the Three Bears."

"Mr. Horza's place? Jesus," said Julian, shaking his head. "This gets better and better."

"Ha. But no. We took a few rooms there so I could investigate what I thought had happened. Look. Talk to Father Ilie. Talk to Ana again. She was there. She'll tell you. It was a strange, horrible thing. But now we are at peace."

"She told me a few things, including what happened with Father Ilie. That's why I'm here. Otherwise I would have laughed my ass off at your request. Or hers, for that matter. Fine. Go to bed. We'll talk tomorrow. And until then, don't even think about skipping town."

"Yes, yes," said Tibi, grabbing the shovel and walking away.

"Wait. What's that?"

"What, this?" said Tibi, looking at the shovel. "I used it to dig here."

"Let me see it. No, don't hand it to me. Hold it up for me."

Julian inspected the shovel with his flashlight for a few dozen seconds. It looked used, just like a normal shovel would, and water was trickling down it, from all the heavy rain.

"I know the model. They have them at all the hardware stores. I have one too. Looks clean."

"Yeah, it is. What, you want to keep it?"

"No. Why? Do you think I should?"

Tibi said nothing for a moment. *Why is he asking me that?* He then had a scary thought. *But what if there are traces of blood on the shovel?*

"If you want," said Tibi, eventually, pushing the shovel a few inches closer to Julian. "I wondered if you'd need it to dig at the site."

"No, no. We have enough shovels. Go home, Mr. Coman, and make sure you stay in town."

"Okay, officer. Goodnight."

"Oh, and Mr. Coman, one more thing," said Julian. "Sleep well. But keep in mind that Mr. Horza is in the hospital and the doctors believe he'll make it. He will be able to corroborate your story, right?"

"Well, he's the one who killed Docan. So, he'll probably deny everything."

"True, true," said Julian, shaking his head. "Goodnight."

* * *

"At last!" said Mia, hugging Tibi as he entered Room 22. "Man, you stink!"

"Yeah, sorry about that," said Tibi, leaning the shovel against the wall.

"Jesus, you look like hell," she added, noticing his haggard face. "What happened?"

"It was a horrible day," said Tibi, "followed by a horrible evening. After our last call, the police came and I've been talking to them ever since."

"What happened?"

"It's a long story. The good thing is, they started digging. The bad thing is, that policeman, Julian, has his eye on me. He's not too bright—he let me keep this shovel—but still, I can't leave the village."

"What's up with the shovel?" asked Mia, looking at it.

"Nothing, I think. He was interested in it, he seemed to want to keep it, yet it was easy for me to make him change his mind. But the interesting thing is," said Tibi, looking at his body, "there isn't a single drop of blood on me. Or on the shovel for that matter. See? Incredible. I was there, soaking in it, but—"

"Where's that idiot?" came a voice, as Mike burst into the room. "Ah, there you are! How are you, man?"

"Ah, hey Mike," said Tibi. "I was just telling Mia what happened."

"Yeah, tell us. You want a beer? Maaan, you stink! Where the hell were you?"

"Actually, can I have a shower first?"

* * *

Tibi came out of the bathroom with a towel wrapped around his waist.

"These are the last clean ones," said Mia, handing him some clothes, "so make sure you don't ruin them before we leave."

"You know, that's odd," said Mike. "I heard that people who eat a lot of meat have stronger-scented sweat. Given that you only eat dandelions, you should always smell like fresh flowers."

"Yeah, yeah," said Tibi, smiling. "What would I do without your snappy insults?"

He sat on the bed and started telling them all about the hole in the waste pile.

"And then, when the ambulance people came, there was *no* hole. Nothing!" said Tibi, shaking his head. "And the toolbox was also gone. And the tunnel I came out of? Gone!"

"Wow! Really?"

"Yeah. It's all very bizarre. Luckily," said Tibi, "I recorded the whole thing," he said, reaching for his phone. "I have a video and some pictures. Wait and see, you'll be amazed."

He fumbled with his phone for a few moments.

"What the hell?" he said, glaring at the screen. "There's nothing here."

"What do you mean nothing?" asked Mike.

"I mean, I pressed Record. I know I did. And I saw the phone recording. But there's nothing saved. Plus, I took a few pictures, but there's none in the folder."

"I tried to call you a few times," said Mia, "but it went straight to voicemail."

"That's strange. At one point, I saw I had full signal."

"The holes weren't there later. Your clothes were stinking, but there was no blood on them. What if you just fainted and fell into a dirty puddle or something? What if it all just happened in your head?"

"Then where did I pull Horza out of?"

"Maybe he was already there, or under that pile," said Mia.

"Or maybe *you* did that to him," said Mike.

"Jesus, again with the accusations?"

"Hey," said Mike, raising his hands, "I'm just saying."

"How could I have done it?"

"I don't know. But all these things you've told us about, all these stories, everything you saw… What if you were hallucinating?"

"Jesus, you really believe that?"

"No, I don't *believe* it. I'm, you know, fearing it."

"Hey, guys, stop," said Mia. "It's a stressful time for everyone. Now, let's all calm down. What happened next?" asked Mia, looking at Tibi.

"You already know what happened next. I called Ana and told her to call Julian, her brother-in-law, the policeman. He pulled some strings and brought the national police to the waste pile. They're looking for the body as we speak."

"And the toolbox? You said it wasn't there after you came out of that hole."

"No," said Tibi. "But it's somewhere in there, that's for sure. They'll find it. And I bet Horza was stupid enough to hide something inside: clothes, murder weapon, I don't know. Enough to tie him to the murder."

"Wow. If that's true, you solved it," said Mike. "That's awesome."

"Yeah," said Mia. "Finally! We can sleep properly and get our lives back."

"I guess. They still need to find Docan's body."

"This damn rain. I see it's at it again," said Mike, looking out the window. "I don't think it will help the search."

"What we know now is that someone really killed Docan," said Tibi. "And that someone was Horza. Then he tried to kill me. And he made the mistake of hiding the toolbox there. Why did he do that?"

"Yeah, it would have been smarter to kill him and then say some red clay boy did it," said Mike, grinning. "I mean, if I ever kill anyone, I won't try to hide the body in a pile. No sir, that's stupid. I will leave it there and blame it on gypsy witchcraft."

Tibi didn't look at him. He took a few steps, stunned, and grabbed the tall backrest of one of the chairs. He started talking, gazing, lost, at the chair he was holding, his voice containing a hint of anger.

"Look, I've also pondered the possibility that I'm the one who did something wrong. But there are too many instances supporting my claims—things that you also saw. For example, Lili heard Snowdrop. The girl already confirmed the blood boy is real. What other proof do you need to trust me?"

"I was joking, man, I'm sorry," said Mike, sighing. "I was trying to lighten the mood a little."

"Yeah, yeah, I get it, you're the funny guy," said Tibi, involuntarily squeezing the chair's backrest, making it squeak under his weight. "But hear me out. Horza was probably scared. He didn't know what to do. He couldn't keep that toolbox with him, so he had to get rid of it, fast. And he chose that dump site."

"Come on, let's go to bed," said Mia, petting Tibi's shoulder. "You need to rest."

* * *

Tibi was walking down the street. He was eating sour cherry pie and red drops were dripping down his chin and onto his chest.

"You ate us," said Docan, next to him.

"But you didn't find it," said Regina.

"You have to find it."

"Find it."

"Find it!"

* * *

Tibi woke, shaking. He grabbed his phone, which was next to the bed, charging.

"Three twenty-two," he said, scoffing. "What the hell?"

"What?" said Mia, waking up. "What's wrong?"

"Nothing."

"Don't tell me you had a dream again!"

"Yeah, I did. I did! And apparently, I didn't find it! I didn't!" Tibi was yelling, desperately waving his arms around.

Mia started crying.

Tibi slumped and stared ahead, not truly seeing anything. "What the hell do I have to find? What is it?" His mind clicked back into gear. "I found that toolbox. I found that shitty blood cave. What? Do I have to go dig for the body myself?"

Mia said nothing, yet she continued sobbing.

He stormed out of bed. "That's it." He pulled on his pants, grabbed the shovel and headed out of the room.

"Where are you going?" said Mia, coming after him.

"I'll solve this, once and for all!"

"You'll go help with the digging? But others are at it. Let them work. They're better equipped."

"You're right," said Tibi, stopping in the middle of the hallway. "But I have to do something!"

His eyes fell on Room 26. Tibi marched over there and reached the door. He tried to open it, but it was locked.

"Do you have the key?"

"Mike has it."

"Fine."

Tibi strode to Room 21. He knocked, violently.

"Aw, what, what?" came a startled voice from inside.

"Mike! Come here! Give me the key to twenty-six."

"What? Twenty-six? Why?"

"Just give it to me!"

"Okay, okay. Hold your horses."

A minute later the door unlocked and a yawning Mike appeared

185

in the opening.

"There," he said, handing out the key. "What's going on?" he asked Mia, as Tibi snatched the keys and rushed toward Room 26.

Mia stood there, watching him silently, her face covered in tears, while Tibi unlocked the door to Room 26. He went inside, turning on the lights.

"Why are we doing this?" asked Mike. "And it's three thirty, mind you. It's the middle of the night."

"I don't know, but I can't take it anymore," said Mia, and a few tears rolled down her cheek.

Within Room 26, Tibi paced like a caged lion ready to pounce. He looked at the corridor, at the doors, then out the windows.

The walls still showed those black spots from the holy water Priest Ilie had used. Nothing seemed to be out of the ordinary otherwise, though, and he turned around. He had the windows to his back now and was looking straight at the opening leading toward the corridor.

"Why are we here?" asked Mike, who had followed him in and stood right underneath the archway. "What's wrong with you?"

"I had a dream. Another dream. Apparently, I didn't find it."

"But you said you found the toolbox."

"Well, that obviously wasn't it."

"And the police will find the body soon. Maybe they found it already," said Mike.

"Yeah, well, I don't know. I just know I didn't find what I should have found," said Tibi, looking at the red wall to his left, where the bed's headboard was.

"I don't know, man," said Mike, sighing.

"Hey, what's happening here?" came a squeaky voice through Room 26's open door. "What have you done to this room? What's with all these black spots on the walls?"

"Oh, Emi," said Mia. "Sorry to wake you."

"You didn't. Some other guests called me about the racket. So, what happened here?"

"It's from Father Ilie's service, the holy water. We'll have to talk about it. But now, now Tibi still feels that—"

"Look, Emi!" said Tibi, taking a few quick steps toward the man. "You have to tell me. What the hell happened in this room?" He grabbed him by the collar, pulling him closer.

"Hey, hey," said Mike, trying to come between them. "Come on, he's not the enemy."

"What the hell happened here?" said Tibi, throwing away the shovel, pushing Mike aside and grabbing Emi with both hands. "Something happened here. I know you know! What is it? What is it?"

Emi said nothing, just looked right, silently asking for help from Mike.

"Hey, man, look at me," said Mike, closing in. "Tibi. Tiberiu! Man, relax. Let him go. Let. Him. Go. Come on."

Tibi slowly unhanded Emi, who took a few steps back.

"Go," whispered Mike, and Emi ran out.

Tibi sat on the bed, facing the yellow wall and the opening leading to the corridor, and started crying.

"What the hell is wrong with me?" he said, as Mike sat next to him, looking away. "What's happening? Why can't I get a break? I've had enough."

Mia came to his other side and hugged her husband, both of them now sobbing.

* * *

Mike said nothing, grabbing and squeezing Tibi's right shoulder.

"And I even assaulted poor Emi. And why? Because he came to check up on what crazy old Tibi was doing, that's why!"

Tibi winced with regret, as Mike sighed.

"I'll go shut the door," he eventually said. "So the noise doesn't… you know."

Mike got up and shuffled down the corridor. As he reached the door, he thought he saw some movement in the lobby, down the stairs. But then he pushed the door closed, locking it from inside.

"Jesus," he mumbled, as he came back.

"What?" asked Tibi, who seemed to be getting ahold on himself.

"Nothing. I thought I saw… nothing."

Mike moved forward, stopping in the middle of the room, looking around.

"Emi is right," he said. "We did a number on this room. You'll pay through the roof."

Tibi kept silent, staring at the floor.

"Jesus, and look at this wall," said Mike, pointing at the yellow one. "When did Father Ilie draw all these crosses? Man, this looks like a room from a horror movie."

Tibi glanced up briefly, then continued to stare at the floor, looking defeated.

"I carved two similar crosses in the cave, to save Horza," he said in a shaky voice, still looking down.

Mike went into the opening and stood there for a moment, arms crossed. He then looked around the room, before walking slowly toward the windows.

"This room is identical to mine," he said to Mia, since Tibi seemed to be lost in his thoughts. "Identical, only mirrored. The only differences are, of course, the colors, and that stupid yellow wall. It's a lot thicker here. Look," he said, trying to make a joke in order to lighten the atmosphere in the room. "It's so wide even *I* could fit inside."

* * *

Tibi wasn't listening. He was staring at the two very large crosses on the yellow wall. They were black, just like the holy water spots, and looked irregular.

"What?" asked Mike, his grin slowly fading. "What's wrong?"

Tibi said nothing as he turned right, reaching for the shovel.

"Hey, man," said Mike, taking a step back. He was a few steps away from the yellow wall and he looked around, probably trying to assess his chances of running. "I don't like that look on your face. What are you doing?"

"They look like they were made by a shovel," said Tibi, moving toward the opening.

"Shit! I knew you did it!" said Mike, taking a few quick steps and reaching the opening before Tibi.

"Done by this very shovel."

"Man! Hey! Don't do it!" said Mike, walking backwards into the corridor while still watching Tibi.

"Tibi!" screamed Mia.

But Tibi ignored her cry. He raised the shovel and swung it.

* * *

The shovel went deep into the yellow drywall, right between the crosses. Tibi pulled the shovel back, and swung again.

Mike was to his left, by the bathroom door, and Mia cowered behind him.

The noise was loud as Tibi's strikes kept falling on the yellow wall. Soon, he'd cut through a large part of it. He squeezed his fingers inside and pulled down on a big chunk of the drywall, breaking it in a cloud of white dust.

And from inside, a large plastic bag fell onto the floor.

Mia shrieked, as the unexpected thud rang in her ears.

* * *

"It was here all along," said Tibi a few minutes later, shaking his head, as they all looked at the body on the floor.

It was in two large plastic bags scotch-taped together. It didn't smell, and the interior of the bag appeared moist and gooey. The bags were dark grey, so luckily they couldn't see through.

"How did you know?" asked Mike, looking pale as he threw glances at the plastic bag.

"The crosses. I made two of them in the cave. And the ones here looked identical. I remembered the cave was dotted with black rocks, just like these spots," said Tibi, moving his hand around. "And the crosses were to the left and right of some white bones. Plus, the walls were all covered in blood, just like these walls are, you know, so red. I mean, the resemblance was uncanny. I think it was a mirror room of some sort. The hell where Docan's soul had been trapped for over four years. But the dream, the dream told me I still needed to find something."

"Weren't you supposed to find the toolbox?" asked Mia.

"I thought so too. They kept on saying 'you didn't find it', but they meant this, the body," said Tibi, pointing at the bags and making everyone look. "They meant this all along."

"Jesus, finally," said Mia, just as Mike grabbed the garbage bin

189

and started to vomit. "Call it in."

Tibi grabbed his phone, looking for Julian's number.

"It's so strange," said Mike, who'd finished vomiting. He took the bin in the corridor, staggering a little. "Why didn't they just tell you where to find the body?"

"Who knows," said Tibi, putting the phone to his left ear. "Maybe they couldn't. Ah, yes, hi Officer Capata. Yes, I found the body. Yes, the body, probably the gypsy. He's in the guesthouse. In Horza's guesthouse, the Three Bears, in Room 26. Yes, I'm looking at it right now. He put it in a plastic bag, then hid it in a wall. Yes, really. Umm, I don't know. I mean, I couldn't say. Could be, maybe. But I don't want to open the bag. I don't think I'm allowed, either. Yes, okay. We're waiting here."

"What was that about?" asked Mike.

"He wanted to know how Docan was killed."

"Why?"

"I don't know. Maybe he wants to link Horza to the murder."

"Yeah, probably," said Mike.

"Should we go to our room? I mean, I don't want to stay here, next to this body," said Tibi.

"Yeah, I want to go," said Mia, in a faint voice. "This makes me sick."

"Yeah, sorry about that," said Mike, clearing his throat as they walked by the trash bin containing his vomit.

"No, not that. I mean, you should have put the bin in the bathroom, I guess. *That* is what's making me sick," she said, pointing at the bag.

Mike reached the door and started unlocking it.

"Ha," he said, as he reached for the key. "I hope Emi doesn't startle me again."

"What do you mean?" asked Mia.

"Last time, when I locked the door, I thought I saw Emi on the stairs, spying on us."

"Well," said Tibi, with half a smile, "he was probably afraid we'd mess up this room even more. And we know he did most of the drywall work, since Horza doesn't know anything about handiwork. Four years ago, when we came here for the first time, he said that he was the only one who— Damn!" said Tibi, suddenly.

190

"He was part of this!" said Mike and Mia at the same time.

"Lock the door! And keep it locked!" said Tibi, grabbing his phone with shaky hands.

Mia and Mike leaned involuntarily against the door, while Tibi dialed the number.

"Damn," said Mike, "that vomit really reeks. Sorry."

"Oh, hello Mr. Capata," said Tibi. "Yes, sorry, Officer Capata. Yes, look. I think you should look at—"

Suddenly, the blade of an axe went halfway through the door, grazing Mike's left shoulder.

Mike was yelling as blood gushed out.

At the same time, Emi let out a cry, pulling the axe out and quickly striking again.

"Mia!" yelled Tibi. "Move away! Come!"

Mia ran as the axe fell the third time, and Mike, too, came back stumbling. He staggered, then rushed past them, directly into the bathroom.

"What?" said Tibi, putting the phone back to his ear. "Ah, yes. Come quickly! We're under attack. Hey, Emi," he yelled toward the breaking door, "I'm on the phone with the police! It's Officer Julian Capata! Yes," said Tibi, this time talking into the phone, "it's Emi! He's also involved in the killing. Yes, Horza's employee. Yeah, the one with the voice. Look, come quickly! He's breaking the door with an axe! We're in Room 26!"

Suddenly, Tibi felt a pressure lifting and his thoughts cleared. He felt as if he'd spent the last few years carrying around a backpack filled with rocks. Now, his shoulders felt light and a strong wave of happiness and hope engulfed him.

"Oh my God," said Tibi, happily. "I think I did it! I think we did it! We did it!"

"What?" yelled Mia, eyes fixed on the door, where the axe fell for the seventh time, breaking a large plank.

"Hey, idiot," said Tibi, confidently. "You know the police are coming, right? We found the body, we found the killers. It was you and Horza. Two idiots. You'll rot in jail, you know that?"

Emi paused, listening to Tibi. Then he resumed his striking, shrilling crazily.

"Run to the other side of the bed," said Tibi, and Mia did as he'd instructed.

"Be careful!" said Mia, as Tibi grabbed the shovel from the floor.

"You," said Tibi, looking at Mike, who stood in the bathroom doorway, pressing a large towel to his wounded shoulder. "Hide in there. Say nothing."

Mike closed the bathroom door and locked it, just as half of the main door broke open, making room for Emi to enter.

"You think you stand a chance?" said Tibi, stepping forward into the corridor. "Don't you know that the whole dream was just about me finding this shovel?"

"What?" said Emi, in his high-pitched voice, halting, looking puzzled.

"The dreams I had. I had to shovel something. This is a good shovel, and it's served me well. It will stop you too."

"I have an axe," said Emi, taking a step inside the long corridor. Tibi held his ground in front of the bathroom door, by the archway.

"I know. Guess what we found?" said Tibi, pointing to the bag on the floor. "Ah, you can't see it from there, but I bet you know what it is."

"Yes, I know. I also know what you're doing. You're just stalling, waiting for the police to get here. Well, I'm smarter than that," said Emi, taking a few quick steps and pushing his axe forward.

Tibi stepped right, through the archway, and entered the bedroom. The bed was a few strides from the opening, and Tibi quickly covered the distance, careful not to step on the body bag. Emi followed him, swinging.

"By the way, idiots, why the hell did you paint this whole room red? Just to make it look like something bloody happened here?"

"No," said Emi in his squeaky voice. "We painted it yellow. It turned red overnight. We painted it over and over," said Emi, his voice getting louder as he waved his axe, "yet it was always red again by the next day."

"Look, put that axe down before you hurt yourself," said Tibi, swinging the shovel wide. It clanged against the axe as they met mid-air.

"So, you knew it was haunted!" Mia yelled. "You bastards!"

"Of course we knew! And I think it was that stupid old gypsy woman. She came a few times, probably looking to steal something," he said, his voice getting higher with every push of his axe, "and she put a curse on us, or on this room. But there was nothing we could do," he added, pressing his axe toward Tibi yet again.

Tibi wasn't trained for sword fighting, so he wasn't closing all the gaps properly. Emi had a few opportunities to deliver decisive blows, but, luckily, he missed all of them. Still, eventually he would find an opening, Tibi realized, and that would be the end of him. And unfortunately, Emi seemed eager to press forward.

As the seconds passed, Tibi's fear came to pass. Emi pushed the axe forward, fast, and Tibi dodged to the side. However, the blade scraped his left cheek, right below his eye.

Blood gushed out, and Emi's mouth twisted upward into a strange, happy grin.

Tibi realized Emi had entered a kind of trance state. No words would make him stop now. No, if he wanted to survive, he needed to act quickly. He needed to take back the initiative.

Tibi moved the shovel differently, striking Emi's axe as firmly as he could. The axe swung to the side, hitting the wall, and Emi lost his balance. This gave Tibi a much-needed window for his next move, especially since Emi's left side was fully open.

Tibi raised his right leg and sprang into a round kick.

Emi was taller, but Tibi was flexible. Tibi's right foot struck Emi's jaw violently, taking him by surprise.

Emi fell instantly, dropping the axe.

Tibi grabbed the weapon, then quickly squatted by Emi and gave him a few quick slaps on the cheek. "Hey, you okay?"

"Oh my God," said Mia, still standing by the balcony door. "I knew you were good at kickboxing, but not like that."

"Come on," said Tibi, smiling awkwardly, "it was just a lucky roundhouse kick."

"Lucky? It was perfectly executed," said Mia, coming closer and kissing him. "Ugh, you're bleeding. Your cheek! It will leave a scar."

"No matter. I'll finally look badass," he said, grinning. "Hey, Mike," yelled Tibi, just as Emi seemed to come around. "How are you in there?"

"I'm fine, I guess," said Mike. "Can I come out?"

"Yeah. By the way, now you understand why vegetarians are

better?"

"Why?" asked Mike, reaching the lobby.

"If I were to eat meat, I would probably be hiding in a bathroom, with an axe wound in my shoulder, hyperventilating."

"Ha, ha," said Mike, turning back to the bathroom and bringing out a fresh face towel. "You're right. I mean it. I'm just pulling your leg with the vegetarian stuff, but it's clear you're in better shape than I am. And probably healthier. Here, use this towel to stop the bleeding."

"So, we did it?" said Mia, squatting next to Tibi and rubbing his back.

"Yes. Yes! I feel free! Like some kind of weight has lifted. I wasn't even aware something was there. Unbelievable," he said, wiping his cheek and then pressing the towel over the cut.

"Wow," said Mia, smiling happily, as they heard the police reach the second floor.

"Jesus," said Julian, coming along the corridor and looking at the broken door. "What the hell is this?"

"That's nothing. *This* is Docan," said Tibi, rising and pointing at the bag. Then he pulled Emi up. "And this is one of the killers. He and Horza did it together. I don't know who struck the blow, what weapon they used, or who came up with the idea in the first place. I just know Emi is the one who put the drywall up, with the body in it."

"How do you know that?"

"He worked on the renovations. He told me so himself. Horza didn't know how to do this kind of work."

"And what's wrong with him?"

"He attacked us with an axe. I'm sure you saw the broken door. And Mike's shoulder. And my face. I had to hit him. Anyway, check that toolbox, when you find it. Now that I think of it, I must have dreamed about it for a reason."

"Dreamed?"

"Yes, dreamed. I told you, ask Ana about all that. Anyway, I bet there's something incriminating inside the toolbox. You'll know who did it. Still, you have this body, and you know whose guesthouse this is. Emi attacked us with an axe. He'll give up Horza for sure."

"I guess so," said Julian, nodding. "Okay. We'll take it from here."

"Yes. Also, please call an ambulance for my friend. He's been hurt," said Tibi, grabbing Mia's hand.

"Of course. But don't you need a doctor for your cut?"

"Yes, I guess I do."

"It will leave a scar, you know," said Julian.

"Yeah, it probably will. I'm dead tired. Is it okay if we do the debriefing tomorrow?" said Tibi, and Julian nodded. "I'll go wait for the ambulance in my room while you guys check the crime scene."

"You'll be even more handsome," said Mia, smiling at Tibi as she checked the cut on his cheek.

"Ugh, I could have died," said Mike, looking at Julian as Mia and Tibi walked slowly toward Room 22. "That hit was critical."

"It was?"

"Yeah. Good thing I was ready for anything. This is like a war injury, you know?" said Mike in a deeper voice, groaning every few words.

Mia and Tibi exchanged quick glances, smiling.

"You'll be fine," said Julian.

"I always thought this was linked to thirteen."

Mia unlocked the door.

"What is?" asked Julian.

"You know, everything. It's Room 26. Two times thirteen, so twice the bad luck."

"Ah," said Julian, sounding distracted, as Mia and Tibi closed the door behind them.

"So, out of all the rooms, this one was most likely to house the body, you know?" Mike's voice sounded muffled through the closed door, and the last parts grew unintelligible.

* * *

A hard knock on the door made them jump.

"It's the medic," said Julian through the door. "The ambulance came; they can see you now."

Tibi and Mia held hands as they left the room, meeting Mike in the lobby.

The ambulance took the three of them to the hospital in the city. There, they treated Tibi's and Mike's wounds, cleaning and sewing them.

Still, everything passed in a blur for Tibi, who was constantly smiling widely.

After that, they insisted on being discharged, and the accompanying policeman drove them back to the village.

"Could you drop us at the Pointy Nose, please?" said Tibi, leaning forward.

"Yes, of course. I'd thought you'd want to go back to the Three Bears."

"No," said Tibi, leaning back in his seat. "I never want to see that place again."

* * *

Once inside the Pointy Nose, Mia locked the guestroom door, and she and Tibi lay on the bed. It was dawn, but they didn't see it.

Mia and Tibi smiled at each other and hugged for a long time, kissing, crying and laughing. They said nothing, just enjoyed the moment, staring deep into each other's eyes.

A few dozen minutes later, they both fell asleep.

And Tibi had the best and longest uninterrupted sleep he'd managed in the last four years.

And it was dream free.

* THE END *

AUTHOR NOTE

This is a work of fiction. All the names, characters, businesses, places, events and incidents in this book are either the product of the author's imagination or used in a fictitious manner.

Some actions and behaviors attributed in this book to the gypsy population have been exaggerated for the purposes of the story.

For example, the ritual described in the "Blood" chapter is inspired by a rain ritual called *Caloian*, which is a ritual not linked to the gypsy people. It is found mostly in Wallachia (now in the southern part of Romania). The origin of this ritual, as is the case with many other local popular beliefs and practices, precedes the spread of Christianity, although it came, in time, to be associated with the period of Orthodox Easter.

Having taken artistic license, no disparagement of the rich gypsy culture is intended.

ABOUT THE AUTHOR

John Black has spent most of his adult life working in the gaming industry and helping create virtual worlds.

He is a gamer, husband, father and pancakes enthusiast. More recently he followed his life dream of becoming a fiction author, writing in the horror thriller genre. His approach to writing is to go all in, keeping it fast paced and immersive.

John likes to think a lot of 'what would happen if' scenarios, and he will continue to explore the genre.

* * *

If you would like to get in touch with John, receive a **free copy** of **Growlers Book 0** and be notified about the release of future books, drop a line at *john.black.author@gmail.com*.

* * *

Readers trust other readers.
If you enjoyed this book please leave an honest review on Amazon. Thank you!

Printed in Great Britain
by Amazon